WHOLLY LAND

C.K. Corcoran

Printed in the United States of America

First Printing 2016

This is a work of fiction. Names, characters, businesses, places, events, and incidences are either a product of the author's imagination or used in a fictitious manner. Any resemblance to actual persons, living or dead or actual events is purely coincidental.

ISBN 978-0692611685

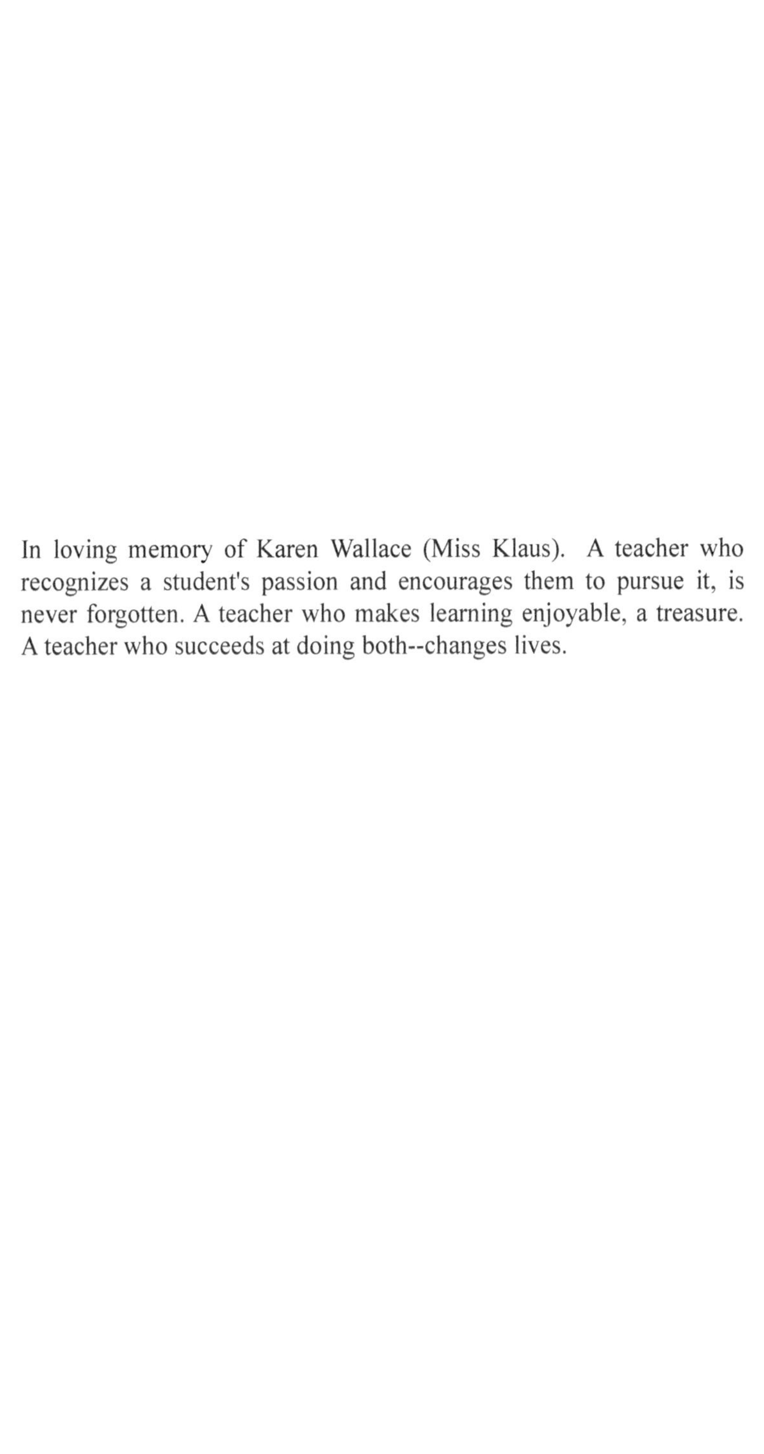

In loving memory of Karen Wallace (Miss Klaus). A teacher who recognizes a student's passion and encourages them to pursue it, is never forgotten. A teacher who makes learning enjoyable, a treasure. A teacher who succeeds at doing both--changes lives.

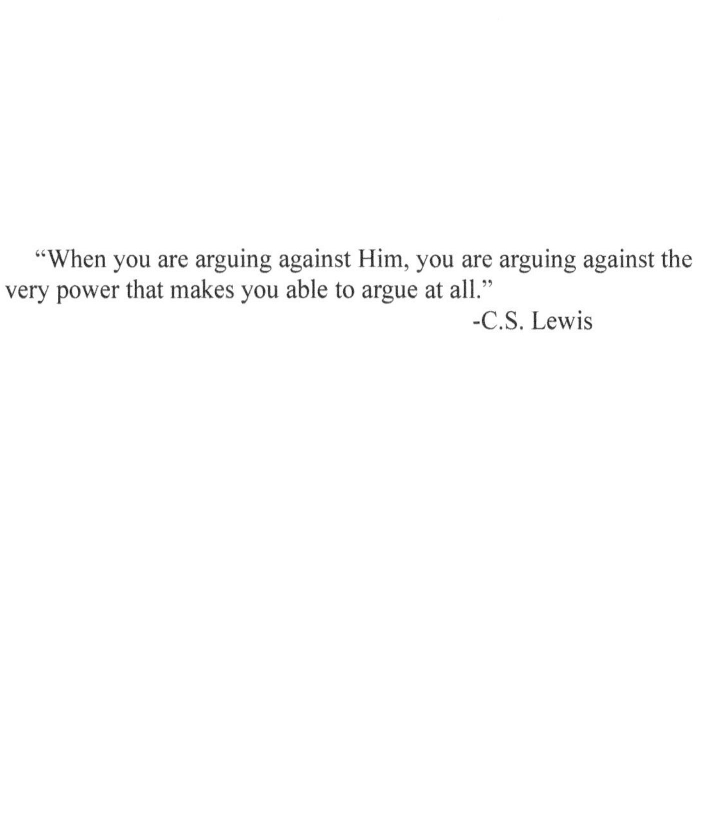

"When you are arguing against Him, you are arguing against the very power that makes you able to argue at all."

-C.S. Lewis

Table of Contents

CHAPTER ONE

The screaming had started again. Kate listened carefully, then turned her attention back to the task of folding the laundry. The screams were not blood curdling and she doubted if her children would incur any life-threatening injuries as a result of the skirmish. Still. She needed to think.

"Cut it out you two! I *mean* it! If I have to stop what I'm doing to come in there…"

It was the fifth time in a span of two hours she used the threat, and since there were at least twenty minutes of quiet in between battles as a result, she decided it was working. She didn't normally raise her voice, but she was at her wit's end. It's not that Kate didn't care about her children's well-being, she loved them very much. She loved them enough to be pairing up their socks and rolling them together just-so. She loved them enough to leave everything they knew behind in California to start over. Kate loved her children. But she was tired...and just a little drunk.

Her life was not exactly the one she had imagined when she was six years old, playing with her dolls. She pretended she was the Lynda Carter "Wonder Woman" doll, getting ready to marry the Lee Majors "Six Million Dollar Man" doll, who would go on to raise happy, synthetic haired children who always got along. For fun, they would hi-jack Malibu Barbie's Van and hit the road to Vegas where they would meet up with the "Tuesday

Wells" doll, who could change her long blonde hair into brunette with the twist of her skull-cap. No. That was not her life. But if she was honest, there were some striking similarities.

Kate did become Wonder Woman, at least, sort of. She *wondered* how she was going to pay the bills, she *wondered* if she would go through with the divorce; because ultimately, she *wondered* if she'd made the right decision to leave him in the first place. *Him*. It was the name she now used when referring to her husband. His actual name was Jared Taylor Swifton Jr. He was not the Six Million Dollar man, but he *was* worth about four and a half million, which was close enough. He took up with a dark-rooted, bleach blonde named Sunny he met at a business convention in Reno. What happens in Vegas, may stay in Vegas, but it didn't take long for Kate to figure out what happened in Reno. She gave Sunny the nickname "Tuesday" for the sake of completing her childhood *doll-adventure parallel universe* and tried not to think about her too much.

"Even Wonder Woman would have signed a prenup," Kate sighed, as she started folding the t-shirts that rolled up at the bottom continuously as if they served no purpose other than to piss her off. She had been in a bad mood a lot lately. She slept little, ate less, and drank more. The quick smile, so ready to give a lift to her friends, welcome people into her home or greet people at the supermarket, had faded. Worry lines crossed her face in a road map manner, the tinier lines branching out like miniature tributaries. The bridge of her sculpted nose and the absent cupids bow of her upper lip showed just how well her surgeon did his job. It was all just a vain attempt at saving herself from getting older by winding up looking

nothing like herself at all. “There is a reason they call it *plastic*,” she'd say.

“Oh, who cares!” Kate scowled, as she stood up and threw the still unfolded t-shirts into the laundry basket. She hesitated, feeling the effects of the Riesling she drank as she folded. “Here I thought a drink would make folding underwear a bit more glamorous. Nope,” she said, slurring her words a little as she tried to regain her balance. Once steadied, she proceeded down the hallway with the laundry basket resting on the hook of her hip. She remembered carrying her children that way when they were babies. Nestled tightly, their legs anchored to her side, they would travel everywhere with her, pulling at her hair with cherub hands and placing slobber kisses on her cheek.

The children were not babies anymore; the oldest, J.T., was twelve. J.T. was *not* short for Jared Taylor, it was *just* J.T. There was no Jared Taylor Swifton III, Kate made sure of that. In the throes of labor, she screamed, “No! I will *not* name my son, *the Third*! I'm not too happy with the *First* and *Second* right now, so forget about another one!” She defended herself by saying if weren't for Jared Taylor Sr. taking her husband out for a night of drinks and carousing a mere three hours before she gave birth, the family's use of suffixes would still be firmly intact.

Her father-in-law used to laugh when he told the story about his distraught son asking the obstetrician, in all drunken sincerity, if there were an on duty priest at the hospital, just in case the subject of exorcism came up. Kate had a natural childbirth, and after twenty-two hours of labor, she reacted *naturally*, “If you *ever* do this to me again, Jared Taylor, I will be holding something *other* than your *hand* during contractions, I swear!”

"I just don't understand women like you, Kate," Jared Taylor's mother cooed, as she held her new grandson for the first time. "I mean, actually *volunteering* for such misery! *I* was put under with *both* of my boys, and I wouldn't have done it any other way."

Kate secretly wondered if her mother-in-law had ever actually woken up, or if she had gone straight from the ether in the delivery room to Martinis at Capistrano's for the next thirty-eight years.

Stella, Kate's six-year-old, was born two months after the purchase of the farmland was final. To hear Jared Taylor talk about it, it was a shrewd investment and a great tax shelter, but Kate knew there was more to it than that. She remembered the day they first found out about the farm very clearly, and after the threat she made in the delivery room years earlier, she was pretty sure it had something to do with fear, as well.

Kate had been in his study looking through real estate magazines while she waited for him to finish a business call. He was having a heated discussion with someone she knew was important, and she knew better than to interrupt. Those phone calls meant money, and money was the lifeblood that kept her husband going. It didn't matter whether he lost a million or made a million, so long as he was talking about it, counting it, or using it for something, he was happy.

As she was perusing the ads for land, she spotted a photo that reminded her of her late grandparent's farm in Southern Minnesota. The feelings it evoked came crashing over her like an emotional flash flood.

What is wrong with you? her husband mouthed, holding the phone away from his ear. Kate shook her head and mouthed back, *Nothing,* then forced a smile and fanned her face to dry the tears as they managed to spill over the levee of her eyelashes. Once she regained composure, she went over the ad again.

100% tillable, making this an excellent opportunity for both developers and investors. Price includes primary residence and several outbuildings. Established fruit trees and new septic.

She glanced up at her husband, who was still talking on the phone, his forehead was furrowed and his eyes were narrow. He held a pen in the same hand as the phone and in the other hand he held his reading glasses. Kate knew, if experience had taught her anything, at least one of the items would be broken by the time the conversation was finished.

"What was *so* interesting, you couldn't get off your ass and tell Amelia to serve breakfast in the study instead of the dining room? I swear, Kate, all the money you wasted on an education, and you can't manage to think your way out of a paper sack," Jared Taylor said as he hung up the phone.

Kate flinched. His words always made her flinch. Even though the vocabulary in his abusive library was very limited, he always managed to use it in such amazingly cutting and creative ways. Her offense? She had not anticipated a half an hour phone call would cause her husband to work up an appetite for an early meal.

How horribly unobservant of me. So sorry, Your Majesty, won't happen again.

"What?" Jared Taylor said, wearing a look of disbelief and anger.

Kate cleared her throat. *He'd heard her.* Try as she might, she could not always keep the thoughts in her head from being spoken out loud. The inability to keep what she was thinking safely between her own two ears, landed her in far more trouble than anything she had ever intentionally said out loud.

"Nothing, Jared, I was just commenting on this real estate ad. It looks like a great place. Wouldn't it be nice if we had a place to bring J.T. when we head back east with you? Someplace he could explore and get his hands dirty, you know? There's so much concrete here."

Kate was just trying to put her husband in a better mood. The *last* thing she really wanted to do was to take the long drive to Chicago with him as they had done since J.T. was a year old. Being alone in a car for that length of time with anybody would make her uncomfortable, but with Jared Taylor, it was especially hard. The amount of invisible baggage she carried with her when it came to her husband, made the drive unbearably crowded. That was how she chose to justify the need for a sedative, anyway. Every Chicago trip started out with Kate calling her doctor about a prescription for Valium. She called it her Dramamine for ***e***-motion sickness.

"Where is it?"

"Where is what?"

"The *land,* Kate! You were talking about the land! What the hell is up with you lately? You're always moody, you're always tired, and you've been eating everything in sight."

"Sorry. Yes, here you go," Kate said. She set the magazine in front of Jared Taylor, excusing herself before he had the chance to notice her tears. It wasn't that the words he said didn't upset her, they did, but she started to cry because what he said was true. Kate knew *exactly* what that meant. She was pregnant. Stella would arrive seven months later. Jared Taylor put a bid in to purchase the farm the moment he found out, and although she was in labor nearly twelve hours longer with her daughter than she was with her J.T.., Kate happily held *only* her husband's hand.

ઉઙ

Having come from the -*you made your bed, now lie in it*- school of thought, Kate didn't feel right complaining too much. Jared Taylor had been surprisingly kind, in her opinion, allowing her to have what she needed the most: *time*. As part of the initial separation agreement, she had the right to stay at the farm for a year before deciding to divorce or reconcile. The once stately home had fallen into disrepair over the years and she was shocked at just how much work needed to be done. The electricity was out in the main house, so there was no pump to provide running water. There was, however, a laundry shed for the field hands situated just a few feet from the back porch that still had power. The situation, while inconvenient, was not impossible. "We'll figure it out," she reassured herself. It took her a moment before it hit her...there was no *we*, everything was up to *her* now, and it thrilled her just about as much as it petrified her.

After she finished putting the clothes away, she wiped the hair from her face, and yelled, "Kids! Bath!" There was silence. They always did this at the mention of the words *bath* or *bed.* Kate smiled, it's not as if she would suddenly forget she gave birth twice, and only two minutes ago yelled at them to settle down. Normally, bath time would mean a quick hop in the shower, soap up, rinse off, and towel dry. That would be normal. There was nothing normal now.

Now, meant going out to the shed, turning on the washing machine and setting it to the hot wash cycle. A washcloth was held inside the tub to catch the hot water, then wrung out and used to scrub off. They also had to be careful to get completely cleaned up before the spin cycle started. Kate had enough problems; the last thing she needed was some paramedic being called to the rescue, asking how one of her kids wound up with an arm stuck in the agitator. There was no steaming hot shower to wash the cruddy day off her skin. Using the washcloth only made it feel like she was rubbing the cruddy in further.

The lack of heat made the waterbed in the master bedroom too cold to sleep in comfortably, so Kate decided to move her things into the guest bedroom. It was the prettiest room in the house, and always ready for *who might come over,* but no one ever did. The irony was not lost on her, as she slipped into the downy envelope of the comforter, the maids had changed the linens on the feather bed and cleaned the room faithfully every week for years, and not a soul had ever slept there. *That she knew of.* In the time it took for her to settle her head onto the pillow, her mind went from zero to sixty with thoughts of Jared Taylor and his mistress racing through her mind. *What if Tuesday and Him had been here* ? Then she remembered why the bed was put in the guest room in the first place,

Jared Taylor was highly allergic to feathers. The thought of her husband running around naked with a full body rash, as a result of the imaginary tryst she was mentally accusing him of having, made Kate giggle, then cry before she finally closed her eyes and went to sleep.

ঙ৪ঌ

The kids were doing okay, although they had changed schools before the quarter was ending, they didn't seem to mind. Although Kate knew they missed their friends and the excitement of the city, they seemed to be adjusting quite well. In California, J.T. had forty other students in a single classroom, here, there were only sixteen other sixth graders in the entire school and Stella loved the attention she was getting as the newest member of her Kindergarten class. She wished she were as resilient as her children.

"*We're good. We'll make it,*" she tried to reassure herself, as she stood at her kitchen window and attempted to absorb what she saw. Though she was not entirely unfamiliar with the word, she still thought "Agriculture" would be a great name for some hipster underground band:

"Live, for one night and one night only, it's AGRICULTURE playing their hit songs: "Soybean a Lot of Fun" and "Who's Herbicide Are You On, Anyway?"

The field reminded her of a vast, dark ocean; the waves of tilled earth were covered with a skiff of snow that could almost pass for white caps. It was early for snow, only mid-October, and Kate was not prepared for the cold so soon. She was thankful the order she placed for winter gear before she left California was on its way. It was not easy shopping for long underwear when the thermometer read seventy-five degrees, but she was glad she didn't put it off. Flannel sheets and shirts, snow pants, hats, and gloves, would be at her doorstep by the end of the week, and she would ask Jared Taylor to bring more clothing with him when he came to see the children on his way to New York. He made arrangements to take them trick or treating. J.T. decided he was too old to go, and since Kate didn't relish the thought of traveling all the way to the nearest city on a Saturday night just for a bag full of sugar, she was more than happy to let Jared Taylor take over that job. He and Stella would go to Cedar Rapids to walk the mall and fill her bag, and J.T. would stay home with Kate to hand out treats to anyone willing to venture that far out on a dirt road for some Milk Duds.

Although the hint of white added some beauty to the otherwise decaying and dark landscape, the weather forecast calling for warming temperatures was good news. The snow would not be sticking around for long. She wondered if she stared at the dirt long enough, she could gain some rurality by osmosis. Eighty acres. She didn't know what an acre was, she didn't even garden, let alone farm. She opened the kitchen window and breathed deep, trying to come up with a name for the smell of the cold air that hit her face.

What little she knew about living in the country came from reading Laura Ingalls Wilder and watching "The Waltons" on television. She never planted a seed in her life. Growing up in a suburb of Chicago did not prepare her for this. Her family warned her years ago, it also made her unprepared for life in California with Jared Taylor. Sure the decision to move out to Los Angeles was the right one, she announced her plans to her mother, who shook her head and said, "Oh well, guess you'll have to learn the hard way, you'll come back eventually."

She did go, and she did come back. Not exactly *back home*, it was a five-hour trip by the time she got on the interstate, but closer than she had been to them in years. She visited her parents and siblings first, before unpacking and settling into a routine on the farm. It was easier that way. Kate did not have time to over-analyze the situation or procrastinate. It was not as if she would consciously avoid going to visit her family, but if she didn't go right away, other things were bound to come up, and she would put it off. Everyone got along well, and as long as she didn't have to spend too much time alone with any one individual, everything was fine. In her opinion, they were much more fun as a collective anyway, and it made it much easier to keep her story straight.

With the exception of her mother, all Kate told any of them, was that she was happily married, very well off, more sophisticated than they could possibly imagine, *and* able to leap tall buildings in a single bound. That was for a grand total of about five minutes. Then she told them the truth. Her version of it, anyway.

CHAPTER TWO

At the gym the next day, with towel in hand, she made her way to the locker room. She looked at the other women in the changing room and noticed the smiles and the laughter as they got ready for their day. Most of them in their 40's, with wide hips, soft bellies, and strong arms. *They* never seemed bothered by all the mirrors in the room. *They* didn't appear to obsess over the fat rolls and the flabby thighs. *They* seemed so comfortable in their own skin. Kate couldn't understand it. *Must be a Midwestern thing,* she mumbled to herself as she toweled off. If any of the women heard her say it, it certainly did not show by their behavior, they continued laughing and chatting away. She waited in the locker room until she was alone, then went about the ritual of looking in the mirror, flexing her muscles and pinching the ¼ inch of fat around her middle as if it were the most disgusting thing in the world.

Before the move, she made sure the town had a gym and she had a membership and directions on how to get there. Right now, it was the only place she could get a hot shower. As a rule, she hated to workout, but she hated the consequences of not exercising more. Kate's PhD certificate from USC hanging on the wall in her study did not get her to where she was, and if she wanted to stay where she was, she had better keep doing those sit-ups. What those would not fix, Botox would.

She married at 29, right after grad school, and had J.T. one year later. Her days consisted of planning parties, soccer practice and doing maintenance work: nails, hair, exercise and anti-aging potions; *maintenance* meant preservation, in the strictest sense of the word.

Leaving the gym, she walked out into the parking lot clutching her car keys just as she was taught in her self-defense class.

That young kid with the John Deere ball cap, hanging out by the station wagon might look innocent enough, but he could also be a mugger, you never know....

Kate was on edge anyway, she was used to having to be wary, to assess every possible scenario. She approached new situations with the same cautiousness she would have if she were preparing to skydive. There had to be a plan and a backup plan. Right now, however, it was as if she were in free fall without knowing whether or not she had a parachute.

Just as she was approaching her car, the cell phone rang. It was *Him.* She even changed the caller ID to reflect his newly given nickname. Even after practicing and practicing speaking in short, direct, sentences so she did not have to engage with him, she was still nervous about trying it out for the first time.

Let it go to voice mail, don't answer, and let it go to...

"Hello?" Kate said, scolding herself.

"Kate?" Jared Taylor said, sounding relieved.

"Yes."

"How are the kids?"

"They are fine."

"I hope you come to your senses soon, Kate, have the children call me."

"Yes, I'll have them call you Thursday."

"Have you found an office space yet?"

"No, I haven't."

"I bet you won't find a thing there, such a Podunk town."

"Yes, I will."

"Kate, you know what? You go to hell."

"Okay, you too, goodbye."

Her hands were shaking as she put the cell phone back in her purse and unlocked the car door. "Well, isn't this just shaping up to be a *wonderful* day!" she muttered under her breath. Once inside, she adjusted the rear view mirror. Kate's failure to put it back in the correct position after using it to check her reflection was just one of the many things she and Jared Taylor fought about regularly.

"How in the world am I supposed to back up when you leave the mirror like that? Honestly, Kate, do you *have* to spend every waking moment staring at yourself?" Jared Taylor would bark.

Suddenly she broke, covering her hands over her mouth to muffle the sobbing sounds. Her index finger caught the tears as they fell and pooled up under her nose, which was dripping by this time. The only thing worse, in Kate's opinion, than the "Public Display of Affection" was the "Public Display of a Nervous Breakdown", and having no tissue at her disposal, she reached into her gym bag, grabbed a pair of clean socks and blew her nose. She sniffled a bit more, checked her mascara, and, leaving the mirror where it was, proceeded to back straight into the white Ford pickup directly behind her.

ଓଃ

Kate yelled as she hit the steering wheel with her fists repeatedly. "No, no, NO!! This did NOT just happen!!" Struggling to compose herself, she pinched her cheeks as hard as she could, it was a habit she had picked up in college to keep her from crying or looking weak. It hurt. It made her mad. But it was far, far, better than crying in front of someone. She reached for the glove compartment containing her insurance information, the skin on her face still stinging. Suddenly, there was a tap on the driver's side window. It wasn't exactly the tapping that startled Kate, though. It was the face of the man *connected* to the fingers doing the tapping. Kate was used to seeing good-looking men, they were everywhere in California, and she had indeed become happily accustomed to it, but this face was different. It was handsome in a weathered, unexpected kind of way. It shook her to see him just standing there, staring at her with a puzzled look. He did not seem angry, she did not feel threatened, but she did not know what to do next. Roll down the window? Escape? What? She did remember she was not to ever, ever, admit that it was her fault, the insurance company would sort it out. Should she call the police? No. If he wanted to, he could. She looked at herself in the tell-tale rear view mirror and entertained the idea of tampering with the evidence just in case they were called, if for no other reason than to avoid any more humiliating conversations with her husband.

Let your speech be always with grace, seasoned with salt, that ye may know how ye ought to answer every man. Kate's grandmother's voice came into her head. *Really? A Bible quote? Thanks a lot, Gran, but I don't think this is going to cut it.* Though it was not the first time it had happened, she was surprised by it. Her grandmother was a woman of great faith, and although Kate loved her with all of her heart, she could *not* understand how in the world she believed the things she did. However, she looked skyward anyway and whispered, "Hey, I know I don't talk to You much, and I'm kind of a horrible person, but could You please do me a favor and help me watch my mouth in front of this man? Amen."

The next thing she knew, her window was rolled down and she was yelling. It was as if she could not control so much as one syllable. The pace at which she swore and the sheer volume of curse words she suddenly had at her disposal was astonishing. She pounded the steering wheel once more and looked up. The man was gone. He had gone back to his truck at some point and Kate did not even notice.

"Great, just great!" she sobbed, as she slammed the car door behind her. Her tears were flowing freely as she headed toward the pickup, which was now at the far end of the parking lot, like an injured animal limping off to be alone to nurse its wounds.

"I am an idiot! I am a complete and total idiot! What was I even thinking moving here? Now everyone is going to be talking about the new divorcee in town who likes to play demolition derby in gym parking lots! Who in the world would ever come to *me* for help with their problems?" The words in her head were running to the beat of her footsteps and she stepped in front of the driver's side door of the truck to *Wait---a---min---ute*?

The man inside was laughing as he wrote down his information for her. Kate stood outside the closed window, waiting for him to respond. She noticed the shaped of his jaw and her eyes traced upward over his lips and nose and she almost caught the color of his eyes, before averting her own. He just smiled and continued writing. *Can he read minds? Does seeing a woman in complete distress make him happy? What kind of a jerk...* He rolled down his window and handed her the piece of paper, touched the brim of his hat and rolled the window back up. She took a step back as the man started the truck up. Before she could think of anything to say, he was gone. Kate, who was usually so good at putting people in their place, the woman with a tongue sharper than a Ginsu Knife was rendered temporarily mute. So she stood there, alone in the parking lot, paperwork in hand and looked up at the sky. *Thanks a lot, God....I bet YOU had a good laugh too.*

CHAPTER THREE

Kate had been on the phone so long her ear started to get hot, so she held the receiver away from her head with one hand and tried to wrestle a peanut butter and jelly sandwich into a zip lock bag with the other.

"Stella woke up with a sore throat today, Jared. She's not going to be able to go trick or treating Saturday."

"Are you feeding her right? Is she getting enough sleep? What about her vitamins?" Jared Taylor asked.

She was not in the mood to be grilled, and the plan to only give him short, direct, answers and not engage in bickering, flew out the window, "Listen, Jared Taylor, kids get sick when they are around other kids, I didn't give it to her! Oh right, I guess it has nothing to do with the lack of heat and electricity. No. It *must* be because I accidentally skipped giving her a *Flintstones*."

"Well, at least you have the hot water from the laundry shed, it could be worse," Jared said.

"*Yes*, Jared, but *come on*, seriously? Can you just take care of it *today*?"

"I'll see what I can do. Kate, what are you going to with the kids once you...*if* you find a space?"

"The kids will be in after school daycare once I get the practice up and running. Before you say it, I *know* why they call it *practice* Jared Taylor, why are you getting so upset? It's not like I'm the one who was unfaithful or anything."

"I'm worried about you; you don't even have any winter clothes for the kids."

"Yeah, right. I bet you are terribly concerned. How was I supposed to know how much it would snow? It's only the beginning of October! I've got a few things here, we'll manage."

"Kate, you *do* know you are in Iowa right?"

"I *know* it's Iowa! I did order winter clothes before I left, they will be delivered here. You know Jared Taylor, if I wasn't so busy hauling hot water in from the laundry shed, I might have had time to peruse the Old Farmer's Almanac!"

There was a long silence, and then they both started laughing hysterically. It was such a sad ending in a way, the only things they had left in common were their children and a strange sense of humor. Infidelity, dissatisfaction and general distrust of each other, had eaten whatever happiness they had left at the table of their marriage. In truth, Kate could not blame the affair entirely for the divorce, it just put it on fast-forward. Kind of like a plant that is dying, and in a desperate attempt at saving it, too much water is added…and it just dies faster.

Kate hung up the phone and looked outside. The black soil covering the field not two days prior, had turned into a blur of gray-white with no visible boundary between the earth and the sky. The fence posts in the main yard were completely bare on one side and battered with snow on the other. So much for the weather forecast being accurate.

She wished she had taken the time to walk the land outside of her home before the snow set in. There was a creek running through it somewhere, she could hear the rushing sound outside her bedroom window at night. She knew she was right to hold on to it for investment purposes, and Kate knew it was now *her house*, but she still felt like a visitor. The handful of times she had gone along with Jared Taylor, she only stayed long enough to shower, sleep and eat some breakfast before continuing the trek east to Chicago. The house itself was rented out most of the year to a local caretaker, who headed up a local co-op that used part of the land as a community farming project to supply the area food bank. The remaining acreage was rented out to a local farmer for grazing pasture.

In just a few years, the value had risen to the point that if they decided to sell, it would bring them a hefty profit. However, Kate was able to persuade Jared Taylor to wait until the children were older; she wanted them to be able to have the experience of vast open spaces and a simpler life.

ଓଃ

Simpler life. Right.

Kate was trapped. After spending an hour trying to get out of her own driveway, she found herself stuck. "Ugh!! How do people *live* like this!" she said, as she went inside to call for help. She walked over to the phone hanging on the wall just inside the kitchen. Taking a deep breath, she picked it up, mumbling to herself, "It's bad enough this old thing is the color of the inside of an overly ripe avocado, but a *rotary? Seriously*?" She could not remember the last time she used a phone book. All of her phone numbers were stored in her cell, but she did not need those numbers anymore. She looked up the number for the towing company and dialed. With every ring, Kate shifted her weight from one foot to the other. She was exasperated, *what was taking so long*? *Did everyone in the county get stuck behind a tractor or what?* As she stood there with the phone to her ear, she grabbed a towel and set it on the floor to catch the melting snow dripping from her shoes.

"Mac's Towing, how may I help you?"

"Yes, yes, my name is Katherine Swifton, I'm at 19823 RR1, and I am stuck in my driveway."

"Welcome to Iowa, ma'am! Sure hope all this snow didn't scare ya too much, it's not unusual to get a bit more of it out where you are at. Don't worry, we can help, you're probably just high-centered. It's going to be a bit before we get out there, though."

"*High*-centered?" Kate exclaimed, "I most certainly am not! I'll have you know I haven't done that stuff in *years!* What does that have to do with being stuck in the snow, anyhow? Is this how you treat all of your customers? How did you know I'm new here? Nevermind, I won't be needing your services, thank you very much." She hung up the phone, shook her head and said, "How presumptuous! The *nerve* of some people, making snap judgments about someone just because of where they're from! Just because I'm from California, doesn't mean I'm some kind of hippie! Why should I care what some country bumpkin from *Iowa*, thinks anyway*?"*

It was only 7:30 in the morning but Kate decided it was too late to go into town. She was too tired and mentally run down for anything more than a good cup of coffee and a cigarette anyway. Since she had quit smoking years ago, she settled on the coffee and sat down and put her feet up on the kitchen table. Instant coffee made with the hot water from the washing machine was a far cry from what she was accustomed to, but better than none at all. She held her index and middle finger in the air and brought them to her mouth and pretended to take a deep, long drag of an imaginary cigarette. She could do that now. It was her table, and she could sit there and blow pretend smoke rings if she wanted to. However, when Stella walked into the room, Kate automatically started waving her hands to clear the imaginary smoke from the air.

"Mom?" Stella asked, looking amused.

"Oh, ya caught me, Stella. Mommy was just using her imagination."

"Mom, if you want to use your imagination, that's okay by me, but if you are going to do *that,* could you go outside, please?"

Kate rolled her eyes and squashed the imaginary cigarette between her fingers and flicked it over her back, then she turned around to follow it with her eyes, and got up and extinguished her *imagination* with the tip of her shoe.

"Yeah, yeah, I got it kiddo. Now, let's find something for your throat."

She gave Stella an old box of Sucrets she managed to find in the medicine chest. Although she doubted the effectiveness of the lozenges, she couldn't find anything else and Stella didn't want to miss her third day of Kindergarten, so it would have to do..

Kate sat down and added throat spray to the running list of supplies that she needed to get at the store. She also made a mental note to check the paper for someone local willing to plow out the driveway on a regular basis. *Wait. Is there a local paper? Where is the supermarket? How will I get to the doctor if I need to?* The only place she had been to was the gym, and she doubted she would go back so soon after the car accident. Her body was in far better shape than her ego, and she was not ready for any more embarrassment.

Reality had just sucker punched Kate square in the jaw, and she felt betrayed. College Psychology 101 set in without her permission as she began to analyze the situation. Clearly, after assessing all of the alternatives, she had made an emotional decision, instead of a rational one. Upon hearing of her husband's affair, she had many other more plausible options from which to choose.

Option one: Kick *him* out.

Option two: Get marriage counseling.

Option three: Sell all the properties, liquefy all assets and with the one-half of the money of which she was entitled under California Law, buy a decent house in a quiet neighborhood and watch her children grow up to be successful, well-rounded adults.

Or, Kate's personal favorite:

Option four: Go Cougar. Take said half, split *it* in half and use it to get major reconstructive surgery on every inch of her body, even taking out the wrinkles on the knuckles of her hands, and go on the prowl for a "new" much younger, *Him.*

Nothing on the list of options mentioned anything about *packing up all of her belongings, grabbing the kids, and leaving her entire life behind in sunny Los Angeles, to move to some farm in the middle of "nowhere" Iowa.*

She stomped the floor with her still bare feet. "*Get me out of this one God, and I promise I'll never…*" she stopped short, brought her feet up to the chair and hugged her legs. The last conversation she had with God in the gym parking lot had not gone so well.

She had more phone calls to make so she knew she could not just sit there all day feeling sorry for herself. Doing nothing would only make her feel worse. Maybe the call to the towing company was just a fluke. Maybe she was wrong about Iowa and was just overly sensitive. She picked up the phone again and dialed the doctor's office.

"Dr. Bauer's office, how may I help you?"

"Yes, yes, this is Kate Swift….ummmm Katherine Brannigan. I'm calling to make new patient appointments for three, please."

"Oh sure, hun, we're open 9 to 5 Monday thru Friday during the winter months."

"Okay. Could I get directions to your office?" Kate was sure she heard giggling in the background.

"Sure hun, we're just down the street from the grocery store."

"Okay, well then…thank you so much, have a good afternoon."

"You too, hun, and if you don't mind me asking, you're the new shrink aren't you? How's your bumper?"

Hanging up the phone with the peals of laughter still ringing through the receiver as she laid it to rest on its hook, Kate sighed. She did not know the directions to the grocery store and was far too embarrassed to call the doctor's office again and ask for them.

ଓଃଌ

Kate Brannigan. Doctor Brannigan. Ms. Brannigan. No matter how many times she practiced using her maiden name, she just couldn't get used to it. Kate had been a Swifton for almost fourteen years and only decided to go back to her maiden name after her mother-in-law told her the rest of the family had requested she do so.

"Just to keep things simpler, and to avoid any confusion or unnecessary entanglements, you understand dear, don't you?" Jared Taylor's mother asked a few weeks before Kate and the children moved to Iowa.

"Sure Margaret, may I still call you that?" Kate asked, blown away at the suggestion of magically making years of her identity just disappear with the help of two lawyers and an "X" waiting for her signature.

"Margaret is fine, sweetheart. I know this is hard for you. Of course in my day, indiscretions came with the territory, women were used to just overlooking such things, but nowadays it seems not all women are suited for such a situation, so let's just try to get through all the unpleasantness and get this settled quickly, shall we?"

Sure. As if *she* had done something to embarrass the family. Though she wouldn't have to officially change her name til the divorce was final she thought she'd better start getting used to it. A bit of resentment still lingered, however, at the thought of having her name revoked, so when a reporter from the local paper called her for the correct spelling of her last name for the write-up on the accident, she just smiled.

"Yes, you have the address right. Actually, no, the last name is not Brannigan. I'm Mrs. Jared Taylor Swifton Jr., yes, that's S-w-i-f-t-o-n. By the way, how did you get my number? I see, thank you. The story made page one? Wonderful. May I get extra copies? Yes, I'll be sending some to my...*relatives* in California. You know how excited people get to see their name in print. Can't wait to share the story with them! Good. Say, .could you give me directions to the supermarket from where I'm at? *Yes*, I've heard of *Google*, my internet is not up yet....great, I'll hold. I'm still here, yes, okay, perfect! Got it! Thank you. Why, yes, I am the new "shrink" in town., and yes, my bumper is fine. Bye!"

"There. Wonder if that's the kind of "unnecessary entanglement" Jared's mother was talking about," Kate laughed as she glanced over the directions to the grocery store. It read: *Grocery—just across the street from Dr. Bauer's office.*

CHAPTER FOUR

It was the first morning since moving in that the family had awoken to sunlight. It found its way through the tatted lace curtains and onto the dusty surfaces of desks and bed stands before spilling onto the hardwood floors. The children noticed all sorts of particles dancing about in the rays running east to west across the dining room. Stella asked what they were, and J.T. replied, "Creeeepy. Dead. *Skin cells*!" as he proceeded to chase her around the kitchen table making monster noises. Kate smiled and made a mental note to check the paper for cleaning ladies. The sunlight did much to lift her mood, and she was starting to warm up to the idea of *here*. Not literally warming up, though. The heater still had to be fixed and the electricity had yet to be restored. She couldn't understand how they had fallen so far behind in the upkeep of the place.

After the children had boarded the bus, Kate gathered the dishes from breakfast and put them in a five-gallon bucket filled with hot water from the laundry room. It made her feel good that she had figured out how to clean with what she had available instead of bemoaning the lack of tap water in the kitchen and using that as an excuse to skip it altogether. Since doing dishes by hand out of a bucket was as close to camping as she'd ever been, Kate started to feel a little adventurous. Her to-do list kept getting longer so she decided a trip into town was in order. She grabbed the phone book and dialed the number to the only realty office listed. She decided it would not hurt to see if she could get some information about any space that might be available for rent.

A smile crossed her face as she watched the circles under her index finger slide over the numbers and back from the small metal hook piece serving as a stop for the dialing plate. She was transported back to 1978 when her family had first put in push button phones to replace the rotary wall phones that hung throughout her parents' house. Her youngest brother would play the theme to "Beverly Hills Cop" over and over on it, annoying her father.

"You know, prank calling is against the law, the person you are dialing can have you arrested it says so right here in the front of the phone book."

Her brother teased, "Dad, who in the world *reads* the *front* of the phone book?!"

All six Brannigan siblings broke out into hysterical laughter, and just as the giggles turned into sighs, Kate's mom started to chuckle silently as if there was a 10-second delay in her *get it?* button. Kate smiled to herself as she remembered her mother, sitting in the rocking chair, trying not to laugh; her small shoulders shaking with tiny spasms, becoming more and more pronounced until a little "hmm hmmm mmmm" could be heard. Then muffled "ha-ha's" would escape her lips, gradually getting louder and louder until it broke in a crescendo of guffaws, which in turn, started everyone else laughing again.

Kate's father, no longer amused, looked up from his reading glasses and said, “That's enough now, it wasn't *that* funny!” Then he went back to reading the paper, shuffling it about as if to straighten the pages, and everyone would immediately settle down.

The "newspaper shuffle"- as it was affectionately referred to, was the equivalent of a judge’s gavel in Kate's family. In the midst of fighting, laughing, cursing, gossiping or anything that made her father feel uncomfortable, it meant “Stop. End of conversation, or I'm no longer interested.”

Kate's engagement announcement was met with the newspaper shuffle. It was also the reaction her father gave when Kate told him she was separating from Jared Taylor and she and the children were moving to the farm in Iowa. When it came to the “newspaper shuffle”, Kate always had a hard time trying to decipher the meaning behind it. When she told her father about the separation, he might have been just hiding behind the newspaper as he:

A.) Rolled his eyes.

B.) Fought back tears.

Or

C.) Looked up to the heavens and said, “Thank You, God!”

Option C would have been a stretch, though, as Kate's father professed no belief in God. He was a straightforward, carve the path of your own destiny kind of guy, and that is exactly what Kate adored about him. Her mother and grandmother were devout Catholics, and Kate's mom took her job to raise her children in the Faith very seriously. That never seemed to bother Kate's father much, though. Kate's mom joked he was only a *situational atheist*. The only reason he said he didn't believe in God was because the only time he could get some peace and quiet was the hour and a half every Sunday morning when the rest of the family was away at Mass.

Out of all six children, Kate was the only one to side with her father on matters of faith or lack thereof. It wasn't that she doubted some kind of divine intelligence existed. It was what she perceived to be the silly superstitions of those who, in her opinion, used God as a scapegoat; blaming God, begging God, or thanking God depending on the situation. Kate was confident if God existed at all, He was not the least bit interested in her trivial issues and complaints, He was probably busy doing the Omnipotent version of the "newspaper shuffle."

CHAPTER FIVE

There is a difference between California sunshine and Iowa sunshine, Kate thought as she struggled to find the pair of sunglasses lost somewhere in her purse. The light bounced off the white snow and just about blinded her. She drove very slowly, not wanting the next front page headline of the newspaper to read: *Local Psychologist Drives Straight into Rural Ditch.*

She remembered the directions from the gym and headed east. She passed by a few brick buildings and kept following the road. After twenty minutes she pulled over, unlocked the glove compartment, and grabbed the *State of Iowa* map, cursed, threw it back into the glove compartment, and headed west for twenty minutes. She reached the city limits wondering if she hadn't made the biggest mistake of her life.

One side of the street was full of two-story brick buildings that looked well over a century old. On the other side, one story buildings with white siding and sheet metal roofs stood like tin soldiers next to each other, the only distinguishing marks being the lettered signs announcing the names of businesses. One storefront had the words

Beauty Shoppe painted in silver lettering and red trim. Kate rolled her eyes, thinking the addition of the P and E and the end of the word *shop* did nothing to make the place look less rural.

Another building held a bakery, with a large blue awning in front with the words *NICE BUNS* printed out in big white letters. It made her smile. "Clever, clever, clever," she mused as she drove through the supermarket parking lot and past the neon *MIGHTY MART* sign. She stopped and shook her head, Mighty Mart was nothing more than a double-wide trailer set on a cement foundation.

She doubled back and headed through town again. She went a bit slower so she could read the smaller print on the two-story buildings. She smiled and said, "Someone in town sure has a sense of humor." A white sign hung down from a green awning with the words :

DR BAUER M.D.
Now Accepting New *Patience*
(because he's done lost his!)

It had been hand painted in black, in some awkward attempt at calligraphy. Nothing else would indicate it was a doctor's office. The signage on the hardware store next door to it bore the same type of lettering,

Cal's Hardware and Pharmacy
We can sharpen your tools and dull your pain while we're at it.

The sudden blare of a trailer truck horn jolted her so much that she veered to the right and braked as hard as she could. She had been driving on the wrong side of the road, trying to get a good look at the storefronts and lost track of what she was doing. She grinned apologetically and mouthed, "I'm so sorry!" to the driver, who looked down at her from his cab and just shook his head, blaring the horn two more times. Kate decided to park and walk the rest of the way to the real estate office, deciding driving in rural Iowa was more dangerous for her than downtown L.A.

She walked past the storefront of "NICE BUNS" and wondered why on this cold day, the door would be open. Suddenly, the aroma of freshly baked bread hit her nose, and like a cartoon character that follows the smell by floating in the air toward its source, she found herself with her nose close to a glass case with donuts, croissants, and other assorted sins, secured safely out of her reach.

A big, deep, voice bellowed behind the counter, practically knocking Kate over in surprise. "Kolaches," said a man donned in a white apron, his face covered in flour. He stood with his hands folded across his belly, smiling broadly. It made Kate nervous. In her frame of reference, a man with his face covered in white like that, smiling like that, would have had her searching for her can of pepper spray. Remembering she was in a bakery, and the white powder was likely flour, she eased.

"Kolaches," she replied smiling, assuming the word must have been Iowan for, *Good Morning.*

"What's good?" she continued, gathering herself up quickly, as she glanced over the counter to see the man who had suddenly caught her, mid-drool.

"Kolaches," he said again, grinning, "You should try a kolach, that's what you need this morning, Doc."

Kate tilted her head to one side, "Doc? I'm sorry, you must have me confused with someone else."

"You're the new shrink in town right? A shrink's a doc, so I called you Doc, get it?" the man replied, still smiling.

She studied him for a second, his dark curly hair and his olive complexion would have her guessing he was Italian. There was something very pleasing about his full face, and Kate imagined he was as kind as he was round. "What's a kolach?" she asked, regaining her train of thought.

The grin on the man's face turned into an "OH!" expression and he held out his arms as he said excitedly, "Wait until you try this," then he disappeared into the back room.

Before she could protest and go through the litany of reasons why she quit eating "poison" long ago, the big man with the white apron reappeared with a paper lined tray filled with dozens of pastries holding a dollop of assorted cooked fruits in the middle.

Unimpressed, Kate ordered a croissant, and the Baker shook his finger at her in admonition.

"No, no. No croissant until you try the kolach."

Kate paused. Ten days earlier, she would have yelled at the man, "The customer is always right, how dare you, I will never do business with you again!" But since she was thinking a bit more rationally, and she realized there were no other bakeries within miles to go to, she accepted.

"Well, okay then, I'll take the one with the red in the middle," she tried to smile. She waited for the man to put the pastry in a bag and let her get on her way.

Instead, he handed her the kolach, then waited; smiling as he rocked back and forth on the balls of his feet, arms crossed, as if to say "See, see, I just *know* you're going to love it!"

So people in Iowa think they can force feed you? Kate thought, looking up quickly at the grinning man to see if he heard her. "Thank you very much," she said, leaving a five-dollar bill on the counter, taking a bite of the pastry as she turned to leave. Two steps later, she back around and holding up one hand, her index finger pointing skyward to signal she was still eating.

"Okay, you got me, seriously delicious. I need to write this down, how is it spelled?

"Sure, doc. It's k-o-l-a-c-h, but some folks add an "e" at the end. Either way, delicious. Oh! I do have to warn you ahead of time, we don't always have them here."

"That's okay, I'll call you first, do you deliver?"

The Baker shook his head, "Nope, get these driven in from Sykora's every Thursday morning, they never last long, so it's first come, first serve, sorry!'"

"So, *that's* how you get loyal customers! Back home we call them drug dealers," Kate laughed. She looked up at the man who just cost her a day's work out. He was clearly not as amused as she was. "I'm sorry, I didn't mean to offend you, and I didn't even catch your name."

"It's Jawolski, but you can call me Wally, and I know you didn't mean anything by it, it's just that I had a brother who got mixed up with the wrong kind of people when he moved over to Chicago, that's all. That big city living just isn't for everyone. Do you miss it, though?"

"I don't think I've had a chance to miss it yet, to be honest. Wait. How did you know I was from California? Jawolski? That's not Italian. I mean, I…don't know what to say. I'm so sorry, Mr. Jawolski, really so horrible!"

"How could you know? No offense taken, Doc…and I'm Czech, actually, but Papa was always giving my mom a bad time when I was growing up about having a fling with Dean Martin because of how different I looked from the rest of the family," he winked at Kate and smiled. "I am glad you are here and if you promise not to tell anyone else, I'll pull a couple of kolaches aside for you on Thursdays and I'll put you on the list of people who are taking the bus to Cedar Rapids for the annual Kolach Festival at St. Ludmila's."

Kate smiled a genuine, heartfelt, smile for the first time in weeks, and she shook the baker's hand.

"Something this good deserves its own festival! Say, you know where the real estate office is by chance?"

Wally smiled, "Right next door, behind the beauty shop, pleased to meet you Doc, and thank you for visiting... *NICE BUNS*! "

He laughed at his own joke, a world away from Kate's; where the remark could have gotten him slapped with a sexual harassment suit. Kate just smiled and walked a little taller as she left the still open door behind her.

A few paces later she found herself in front of the beauty parlor and opened the door. The smell of ammonia was overwhelming and she covered her nose. She wasn't sure if it was the smell or the sugar rush, but she felt faint and reached for a chair and sat down, putting her head between her legs. After a few moments, she raised her head and was met by three concerned looking women, one holding a glass of water, the other two attempting to fan her with their hands. The woman holding the water bent down and offered it to Kate.

"Here dear, drink this, I'm Carla, I should have put my "permanent in progress" sign on the door this morning, I am so sorry! That ammonia smell can really get ya and we don't have the best ventilation system here." As Kate regained focus, she thanked Carla and took a few sips of water.

"My name is Kate," she offered.

"Nice to meet ya, I'm Maeve," said a stocky redhead who looked to be about 50, the first signs of sun damage making itself visible around her dark brown eyes.

The other woman stood back, with her hands on her wide hips, pursing her lips. "Carla, my head's burning, let's get these out!" she said as she sat down in the big padded chair, trying to fit her thick neck into the curve of the rinsing bowl.

"That's Charlotte, she's been to California once," offered Maeve, as she maneuvered her large frame into the seat next to Kate. The arms of the chair disappeared under the parts of her that didn't fit as she spilled over them. "Here you go, you have a little…" she said, as she held up a napkin while making circular motions around the corner of her own mouth before handing it to Kate.

"Oh, shoot! Thanks!" Kate said, before wiping her face. "I was next door and had breakfast, guess I left some here. Maeve. That's Irish, right?"

"Yes, yes, it is!" Maeve looked like she were about to burst; her eyes got bigger and her hands became more and more animated, like she was conducting some imaginary symphony. "Not many people know that. I knew you were smart, no matter what anyone else said about you! My great-grandfather purchased seventy acres about ten miles from here when he left Ireland. I'm still on the land, although I don't farm it anymore. I take care of my dad, he lives with me, or I live with him...anyway, it's all about family, you know? I didn't want to put him in a nursing home, he's been all by himself since mom died a couple of years ago."

Kate tried to keep up, with Maeve's speech, but only caught bits and pieces: *single, works at the deli, likes Coors, and Spaghetti Westerns …*

"How about you, Kate, what brought you here from California?"

Kate was not about to get into her life story with this woman. Not today. Not ever. There was something about her that made Kate feel uncomfortable. Maeve seemed too genuine, too likable. Kate did not move from California to make friends in Iowa. She left L.A. to get *away* from complications, not to make new ones.

"Oh, it's a long story, and I really need to get going, I'm trying to track down the realtor about any open offices for rent."

Maeve let out a loud laugh, "Kate, you've been talking to me now for 20 minutes! C'mon, I think I have the perfect place!" She grabbed Kate's hand, startling her, and Kate recoiled.

"Oh, oh, dear! I am so sorry! No one told you I was the realtor?" Maeve apologized. "My nickname is "Maeve O'Manyhats," she laughed. "In a small town like this, we have to cover a lot of bases. I didn't mean to make you uncomfortable, we can stay here if you like."

Kate, still trying to figure out how she went from talking to a cashier who drank beer and collected baseball cards, to the realtor who she spoke with earlier in the day. Whether it was the peroxide, the sugar, or the way Maeve got into her space, Kate wanted nothing more than to get out of there, go back home and hide under her covers until the world made sense again. Instead, she nodded and said,

"No, no, of course not, let's go, I was just surprised." She turned to Carla, said goodbye, and then followed Maeve out the door.

CHAPTER SIX

Maeve's office consisted of a large oak desk and a filing cabinet with a coffee pot, containers with cream and sugar and a stack of yellowing Styrofoam cups on top of it. The room reeked of stale cigarettes, and Kate found herself saying "yes" when Maeve offered her one from her pack. "I didn't think it was legal to smoke in public buildings," she said casually as she shook her head "no", and continued, "I forgot for a moment, I quit years ago."

"Oh, it is, but this isn't a public place. It's my private place and in my place, I'll do whatever I darn well please," Maeve quipped. "That is to say, when I'm just here by myself, I mean, I can take this outside if you like."

Kate motioned to Maeve's chair "Don't be silly, sit down, let's take a look at what you have for office space rentals."

After two hours of talking, and a half hour of touring the vacant offices in town, Kate decided on one. She did a mental eeny meany miny moe in her head to choose, as both spaces were nearly identical except for a window facing the gym in one office, which made Kate smile for a moment and taking the keys from Maeve, made arrangements to set up the next day for moving. "Might as well get on with it, I don't have much in the way of office furniture right now, any place you recommend?"

"*Ask and you shall receive, seek, and ye shall find.*" Kate heard the verse her grandmother used to recite often. "*C'mon Gran, I don't think your God really cares if I find furniture that will fit my budget. Besides, "world peace" seems just a little bit more important right now.*"

"World peace? Sure. That's important too, but with all due respect, Ms. Brannigan, I don't think our Heavenly Father would begrudge a single mom trying to make ends meet, a good deal on some office furniture."

"Oh, for goodness sake, did I say that out loud?" Kate's face turned crimson. "When I get stressed out, I am reminded of some of the things my late grandmother used to tell me. It brings me peace sometimes. Other times, well, it is pretty embarrassing, especially when it seems like I'm talking to myself. I'm sorry about that."

Maeve just laughed "All I have to do is go home, and there's Pops, sitting in his La-Z-Boy, ready always to dole out kind advice and helpful criticism. Don't worry, I *get-cha*, Kate. Okay now, there's plenty of odds and ends, maybe a desk and a few chairs in the building's storage area, and that I'll make sure the office is at least partially furnished if you want to go through it and choose what you like."

Remembering that her new budget was hardly what she was used to, Kate readily agreed.

She arrived home just in time to see the children off the school bus, and they all raced to the porch door with gloves and scarves in tow.

"Mom. Why do you carry your mittens, when it is easier just to put them on because it's one less thing in your hand, you know," said J.T. in a voice that sounded just a little too familiar to Kate. She almost turned around to reprimand him for his tone but thought the better of it. It had been a good day, and Kate refused to ruin a perfectly good day with a few harsh words.

"Gosh, J.T.! Great idea!" she said, and the three fell inside the door at the same time, spilling backpacks and galoshes all over the entrance of the enclosed porch.

"Okay guys, let's get some dinner, I'll order out...oh, I forgot. There's nothing that delivers out this far. Darn. Not even a drive through if we were to go back to town. Sorry kiddos, gonna have to settle for what we have here," Kate said. The thought of loading everyone into the car and driving all the way into town just to shop at a double-wide trailer made Kate cringe. No, there must be some peanut butter and jelly left in the pantry. The kids wouldn't mind, and since Kate had already eaten the kolach this morning, she figured her diet was off for the day anyhow. She smiled, feeling oddly relaxed. Was she starting to feel optimistic? No. Not yet, but she did feel, for the first time since their arrival, that perhaps this move wasn't as big of a mistake as she feared it would be.

She flipped up the light switch, as she had done out of habit every single night since they had arrived, only this time it worked. She and the children cried out in unison, "Lights!" Finally. Could that mean a hot bath on top of the already decent day? Did she dare? Turning on the left faucet, she waited. Water! Not too hot, but it must take some time for the water heater to warm it all…she did not care. It was working! A late hot bath was better than none at all, and the kids would be happy to take a quick lukewarm shower after the washing-machine-water washcloth baths they had been putting up with.

The kids were both exhausted, playing in the snow every chance they got at school. They had never had the chance to "play" in the snow, not seeing much more than a dusting of it in their lives. Kate eagerly listened to every detail of their cold weather escapades. They had built three snowmen, two igloos and had three snowball fights during recess. She was so happy that they were happy. She started thinking about the difference between children and adults when it came to the white stuff. She wondered when it became a bother instead of a wonder. The snow became the enemy when it stood between her and getting what she needed to get done. When she had no such responsibilities, it was paradise.

Perspective, is that what it boiled down to? Could it really be that simple? Kate hoped she could change her mind about this place, about her marriage, about a lot of things. Reaching into her purse for her lip balm, she felt a folded piece of paper and gasped. She had forgotten all about the insurance information that "Pickup Truck-Man" had written:

Don't worry about the truck, I get the feeling you have enough to worry about right now, considering the reception I just received. I'll get it taken care of. Just breathe easy and relax, you're not in California anymore, darlin'. I am sure we will "run into" each other soon, maybe I can "hit you" up for a cup of coffee when you are settled in.

There are extra food supplies behind the wall on the left side of the pantry. Just pull out the can of garbanzo beans on the third shelf, there's a little hole in it, hook your finger into it and pull. There's some canned tuna, crackers, and I think there may even be chocolate, who knows, it may be just what the doctor ordered. -Sawyer

Kate dropped the note and put both hands on the table to steady her. Her head was spinning. Who *was* this man? How did he know that there was hidden food in the pantry? *She* didn't even know about it. The thought of some stranger wandering through her house when she wasn't home sent her into a tailspin and she picked up the phone to dial 9-1-1.

"9-1-1, what is your emergency?"

"Ummm …."

"This is the emergency dispatcher, what is the nature of your call, please?"

"Well, you see…"

"Ma'am, we have you listed at 19823 RR1, is this correct?"

"I'm not sure, but it's just that…."

"What is it, Mrs. Swifton, do you need an ambulance or sheriff's deputy to come out to your place?"

"*Mrs. Swifton*? Where did you get that information? How do you know it's me? I mean…"

"The name comes up on the caller ID ma'am, now unless you tell me what is wrong, I will send one of the officers out to talk to you."

"Crud."

"Ma'am?"

"Okay, deep breaths, Kate, deep breaths."

"I'm sorry, Ma'am?"

"Sorry, I was talking to myself. I have a note...a man I do not know has been in my house while I was away. I have it in writing, you see I am very concerned for my family's safety and I…."

"Ma'am, are you talking about Sam Sawyer?"

"What kind of place *is* this?! Just tell me who this guy is, so I can have him arrested for trespassing. "

"I don't appreciate the tone ma'am, and according to our records, he is a renter on your property."

"That can't be, you don't understand, how do you have access to all this information anyway? I was never told about this. My husband never said anything..."

"I suggest you check the rental contract concerning this matter tomorrow, and ma'am, if you don't mind me saying, maybe this is something you and your husband should discuss."

Kate tried to put the phone back on the hook and missed, the cord was wound tight enough that it kept it from dropping to the floor and Kate just stared at the receiver as it started its slow unwind, gathering speed just as she picked it up to slam it into its place on the wall. She looked around in dismay, "What in the world have I gotten myself into?" she whispered, before sitting back down, exhausted. She fell asleep at the kitchen table, using her arm as a pillow, her sleeve catching the tears that fell even as she dreamt.

CHAPTER SEVEN

Kate awoke to a very excited Stella yelling, "Mom, mom-mom!" The enthusiasm she was greeted with grated on her. She was just dreaming about leaving a party late one night when she was younger. In it, she and a date had just left a swanky New York reception at 740 Park Ave and her suitor was talking about his plans to live there one day. "Someday, just you wait, *I* will have a place in that building. *I* will have power, *I* will have riches, and *I* will ..." (SLAP!) Kate cut her escort short. Still heady with the evening's excitement, she struggled to maintain herself in a lady like way. The poor fellow at the other end of her hand rubbed his jaw for a moment and said "I know in *this* building, no one just "gives up" their power...but we are young and WE are beautiful…" (SLAP!) Kate meant it this time. She was unsteady on her feet and slurred as she spoke. "Oh, you poor, miserable man! For gooonessakes!"

"Mah ahh *UM!*! It's Saturday, it's Saturday! Daddy's coming! Daddy's coming!" Stella said, shaking Kate's arm, as she jumped up and down.

Kate groaned, it really was a dream, the only time she had seen Park Avenue in reality was on a Monopoly board.

She rose up slowly, her neck stiff and her mouth spilling drool from the pool inside of her cheek.

"Stella, it's Friday, and Daddy isn't coming." The annoyance in her voice surprised her a little. Kate liked to think she could maintain her composure, at least in front of her children. Single motherhood was a far cry from the life she was used to. Everything was on her now, no one else was there to bear the everyday responsibilities. She wondered how in the world other women did it. As far as support from her family was concerned, Kate did not bother to ask. Divorce was not a subject brought up in dinner conversation and certainly not something her family approved of.

She recalled the talk she had with her mother just days before she and the children headed out from California,

"Have you at least considered counseling?"

"Mom, I'm packing, like, *right now*, so it's a little late for that."

"Well, I just wish you would have called us sooner before it had gotten to this point."

"I'm sorry mom, didn't mean to ruin the family's perfect track record."

"You know that's not what I meant."

"I know, I'm sorry, but I don't think there would have been much anyone could have done."

"Maybe not, but we could have at least prayed for you."

"I thought you did that anyway, what, you don't light a candle for your wayward daughter at St. Thomas' anymore?"

"Now you know that's not what I meant, Kate, stop being so ugly."

Kate looked at herself in the mirror...it would take twelve more hours of sleep and a spa day to keep her from being ugly at that point. Her mascara was still smudged from a crying jag the night before, her lips were cracked and dry, and her disheveled hair hadn't seen a comb for two days.

"I'm sorry mom, I didn't mean to take it out on you. Listen, I'll call you when we decide what we're doing, I'm pretty sure I'll be moving out by the weekend. Thinking of taking the kids to the farm for the winter, just until we can work out what to do next."

"Do you think that's a good idea? You'll be out in the middle of nowhere."

"Mom, I'm in the middle of *everywhere* right now, and it's suffocating. Honestly, I think it will be a welcome change. I'll stop to see you before we move in. It's really only a few hours difference and I would rather see you and dad first. Okay, talk to you later, love you." It was normal for Kate to end the calls with her mother like that. If she was ready to hang up, she didn't dare allow one moment for a word in edgewise.

Stella tugged at Kate's sleeve, snapping her back to reality.

"Mom? How are we going to go trick or treating? Can I talk to daddy?"

Kate sucked in her breath, the kids hadn't called their father and she was to blame. The shock over the pantry note caused her to completely forget. There was no nanny anymore to take care of those small details Kate often forgot, and no husband to blame anymore when she didn't remember the big ones.

"Listen, sweetheart, daddy has to wait until before Christmas to come, but he can come and help you pick out just the perfect Christmas tree, so we'll dress up for Halloween and hand candy out here, okay?"

Stella's eyes began to well up with tears, but she swallowed hard and said, "Well, today is show and tell... what can I bring?" Kate thought about tearing the wall phone out and throwing it in the backpack, but Stella settled on a still unworn pair of pink cowboy bootswith her initials branded on the back.

"Daddy says I should ask you for a horse!" Stella cried as she held the boots and clopped them up and down on the table.

"Oh, really? That's funny, he never mentioned it to me." Kate laughed, as she scooped the boots away mid table-gallop.

"Well, he did. He said you are going to have cows and chickens and a big, old, ass."

"Stella!" Kate exclaimed.

"What? J.T. says that ass is just another name for a donkey. Did you think I was talking about your b-u-t-t?" Stella started giggling so hard she bent over.

It made Kate smile to think her child could say one word without hesitation, and yet still be innocent enough to think the other word had to be spelled out.

"Please stay just the way you are, kiddo," Kate said as she leaned down to give her daughter a kiss.

"You stay the same too, mom," her daughter replied as she boarded the bus.

"Let's hope not, sweetie, let's hope I can change a *lot*," Kate whispered as she waved good-bye.

CHAPTER EIGHT

There was a slowness about the town that bothered Kate. She was having a terrible time adjusting to not always being in a hurry. So when the phone to the doctor's office had reached its tenth ring, she started to hang up, but remembered there was no such thing as "redial" on a rotary phone, so she stayed on. Finally, after ring fifteen a voice greeted her:

"Dr. Bauer's office how may I help you?"

"Yes, this is Kate Brannigan and I was wondering..."

"Oh! Hi there, Ms. Brannigan, she won't be in until 11:15."

"What?"

"Maeve.... that is, that's what you were wondering about, right? She said she would meet you here at 11:00, but she's running a little late."

Kate was afraid to say what she was really wondering at that point so she decided to just to let it go. "Oh, yes, that will be fine, I don't think I even caught your name, I'm sorry."

"It's Elizabeth, but you feel free to call me Lizzy, okay? Are you settling in okay out at The Piper? Hope you can stop in after you meet with Maeve, the girls here in the office are excited to meet you! We have some office warming presents for you if you get a chance."

The phone slid down the front of Kate's throat slowly, to the safety of the crook of her neck before she picked it up in a daze. What in the world was "The Piper"? How did everyone in town seem to know more about her life than she did? She did not remember sending a press kit to the Chamber of Commerce if there was one. She laughed out loud, picturing the owner of "Nice Buns" moonlighting as the president of the welcoming committee,

"Visit for the atmosphere, relocate for the kolaches"

It was exactly 11:15 when Maeve showed up in front of the doctor's office looking disheveled and a little tipsy, Kate was shocked when the girls at the physician's office did not seem to mind a bit when she came through the door to greet Kate.

"Well, well, look what the CAT-sup dragged in...ha! Get it, I said Catch-up instead of," Maeve hiccupped and turned to the receptionists. "Hi girls, I'll be back down in an hour and tell you ALL about last night!! C'mon, string bean, let's get you settled in, shall we?"

As Maeve went to grab Kate's arm, the look of astonishment Kate unsuccessfully tried to hide, caused her to pause. Collecting herself and shaking her head she said, "The girls didn't tell you, did they?"

What girls? Who was she talking about? Kate searched for a point of reference and then began to put the pieces together too slowly for Maeve.

"Okay, I'll tell you! It was my pre-birthday party last night!! *Woohooo*!" Maeve circled her index finger in the air and tried to make the sound of a cork popping with the other index finger. The act must have required more coordination than she could muster and she stepped backward and plopped on the stairs leading to the office instead.

"Oh, happy birthday, Maeve, I didn't know. Are you sure you are okay to go up those stairs?" Kate caught herself mid giggle and cleared her throat.

"Birthday? It's not my birthday, silly! I said *pre*-birthday," Maeve said, amused with herself. "My Birthday is in January! I can celebrate with a pre-birthday party 325 days a year!"

Kate did the math in her head and gave Maeve a puzzled look.

"I give up drinking for Lent love, that's 40 days, now let's get going!" Maeve instantly appeared sober as a judge, and directed Kate up the stairs, past her new office and to a landing that held a plethora of used office furniture.

"There's so much to choose from!" Kate exclaimed, eyeing the leather office chair with the brass buttons.

"They are yours for the borrowing, Kate, everyone used this landing as a storage place, actually, most of it is donated from old Doc Martin's office when he died, no one wanted to sit in the furniture once he passed...big shoes to fill, those were," Maeve mused.

Kate waited to see if Ashton Kutcher was behind the door to tell her she was being "punked"-- *Doc Martin*? *Big Shoes*? Seriously? When no celebrity appeared to tell her she was part of a prank, Kate stepped up onto the landing and began her selection. She decided to take the fainting chair, oak desk, table lamps, love seat and the leather office chair.

"Who is going to help us move everything?" Kate asked.

"Who do you think will help us move?" Maeve looked surprised. "Well, we can get most of it, and I suppose I can call on Sawyer, he'll round up a couple of the high school boys to help with the heavy stuff."

"Sawyer?" Kate's mind raced for the right words to finish the sentence. *The creep who comes into my house when I'm not there? The man who had me so distracted trying to remember the color of his eyes, I had to settle for a cup of hot water because I forgot to put coffee in the filter before I turned the pot on this morning? That guy?*

"Who's Sawyer?" Kate asked, trying to sound non-nonchalant. She kept her head down and began nervously prying at the brass buttons on the office chair with her fingernails.

"You know who Sawyer is, Kate! You backed right into him last week! He wrote you a note telling you where to find the extra goodies! Sorry about the missing chocolate, there's one left, I think. I was out there helping a few months ago and," Maeve rolled her eyes and slapped at Kate's hand, "and stop messing with those buttons! That chair is an antique!"

Kate lifted her hand from the chair and wiped the hair from her face, catching bits of perspiration as she drew it back. She could feel her face getting flush, and she stood there, silently begging Maeve to change the subject.

Maeve continued, "Sam Sawyer, I've known him forever, he has been taking care of The Piper for almost thirty years now. If there were ever a man with a heart of gold, he's it. He's the one who convinced that husband of yours to keep the name of the farm, it used to be the airport in town when we had one. You've heard of a one-horse town? Well, ours was a one plane town."

Kate started throwing sheets back on the furniture she did not want. "Let me guess, the plane was a Piper?" she smiled.

"And everyone said Californian's brains were made of granola! Sawyer also managed to keep the community garden and Farmer's Market going, at least for this year, unless of course," she shot Kate a dirty look, "you decide you don't want it to continue. The poor man has been through it, you know, after all, these years, he still goes and visits his wife most every Wednesday and sometimes he'll stay over on the weekend, so I'll have to talk to him about when he can help and let you know."

Poor Sawyer? Wife? What? Kate moved to the front of the office chair, fingers clutching the side as if to prevent a fall, and sat down, hoping what she was thinking would stay in her head and not come out of her mouth.

"Oh, mercy sakes! Let me get you some water, you look like someone could knock you over with a feather!" Maeve insisted.

"No, no, I'll be fine, I just felt woozy for a moment, let me sit for a second and then we'll get some of the smaller things moved in, okay?" Kate brushed off the offer of water, although the inside of her mouth was as dry as cotton and the look on her face betrayed her attempt at trying to hide how she was really feeling.

"Was it something I said? Me and my big mouth!" Maeve leaned in to feel Kate's clammy forehead.

Kate waved Maeve's hand away and put her arms to rest on the chair and straightened her back. "No, no, it's just...I didn't know..."

"Didn't know Sawyer had a wife? My goodness, I can't imagine why you would, Sawyer rarely ever talks about her. I can tell you he hasn't been the same since, and well, you'll have to forgive him for not wanting to speak to you after the accident the other day. He just found out that she'd taken another fall and he wasn't quite himself."

"Excuse me, Maeve, but that is none of my business, I was just wondering how he knew so much about our property, and you gave me more than I want or need to know." Kate cleared her throat and swallowed hard, then tried to bring up enough saliva to keep the inside of her lips from sticking to her teeth.

Suddenly she got up, pushed Maeve aside and ran down the dark hall to the bathroom. Kate felt dizzy and clammy and all she wanted to do is go back to California, tail between her legs and beg Jared Taylor to take her back. She was sure she was losing her mind.

A few seconds of running cold water over her wrists and splashing some over her face brought her back to her senses. "What just happened in there?" Kate asked the reflection staring back at her. "You spend a couple of weeks in the Midwest and you let yourself fall apart over a man you don't even *know*? A grizzled old cowboy wanna be? This is Iowa! Farmers are in Iowa! Cowboys are in *Texas*!" She hit the sides of the porcelain sink with her hands and said to the mirror, "You have got to get it together!" The embarrassment she felt was almost enough to keep her locked in the bathroom, but she knew her reaction went unnoticed by Maeve, or the cause of it anyhow. She wiped the black mascara that found its way down her cheek and went back out to find Maeve.

Kate noticed the smaller pieces of furniture had already been moved into her office as she walked by it on her way to find Maeve. "Hey, you don't have to move all of this yourself, I'll be right there, just got your hangover by proxy, I think. I'm much better now."

"You must be a wine drinker, darlin', I haven't had a hangover since 1980," Maeve shouted. Then broke out singing at the top of her lungs: "*Ohhhhh...* Gin' gives me the spins and it ain't my friend, the fruit of the vine takes too much time, but two or ten pints of some cold Guinness Stout, *THAT*, is what it's all about." Then Maeve laughed, the sound bouncing off of the strange angles in the hallway before landing on Kate's ear causing her to sound like she was talking through a megaphone. Kate laughed, "Alright then, alright then, I give...you win...besides, don't you have a pre-birthday party to get ready for?!

"Ah, you see Kate, just because I said I *could* celebrate, doesn't mean I *have* to," Maeve said indignantly. Perhaps you should get to know me better before jumping to conclusions, okay? Alrighty then. C'mon, let's go downstairs to Doc Bauer's for a beer."

Kate smiled and followed Maeve down the stairs with a look of morbid fascination at the thought of going to an "office warming party" at her doctor's office where there was a 12 pack of Coors Light stored right next to the penicillin.

CHAPTER NINE

The phone rang at 11 p.m. Kate, exhausted from the day's activities, had fallen asleep on the couch with a quilt that had been in the house since they first bought the property. It was handmade by her grandmother and had been the piece of her childhood she could envelop herself in when she needed to. She inhaled the worn fabric as brushed up against her cheek. Sometimes she swore she could smell the cold autumn night mixed with the aroma of hot cocoa and the vendor popcorn from the high school football games she attended with her grandparents on her trips back to Minnesota. It was cumbersome and too big to be folded correctly, so it had stayed at the farm because there was really no use for it in California. Kate decided the reminder of her grandmother was destined to be appreciated in Iowa, where it actually got cold enough to use it. She smiled when she thought of the *home away from home* she rarely stayed at all these years, becoming her *home-home*. She let the phone go on ringing, then remembering she had no message service set up, scrambled to pick it up.

"Hello?"

"Kate?"

"Yes, who did you think it would be Jared, why are you calling so late?"

"I....I.... Just missed your voice."

"Look, we've been over this...and I don't want to stay up all night re-hashing it again. Jared, you have got to stop, we'll talk more when you get here in person to help Stella with the tree."

"About that..."

"No way, Jared! Don't tell me you're backing out of this one too!"

"It can't be helped, I'm stuck here on business, you'll think of something won't you?"

"Of course, Jared, I always think of something. I just wish you would start thinking for a change."

"Excuse me? What is that supposed to mean? You were the one who left, remember? You were the one who broke up our family by taking off. You were the one who never even gave us a chance."

"A *chance*?! What kind of chance did I not give you, Jared Taylor? Stop sleeping around, please. Tell your mother to mind her own blessed business, please. Tell your father to quit looking down the front of my blouse, please. Tell me, those weren't chances that you threw away? And while we're at it, how about the nanny that you chased away because she wouldn't sleep with you. Or maybe the maid who always cooked dinner early when she knew you'd be home so that she could leave before you got there. Hmm, Jared, you don't think I gave it try? You don't think I gave it the ol' fighting chance?"

Kate waited for an answer. She didn't know why she didn't hear the phone disconnect, but she was yelling to no one. Jared Taylor had hung up.

She wanted to be angry with him. She wanted to be so mad that she would throw stuff and break things. But she wasn't and she didn't. She was too angry with herself. When Kate thought about the list of signs that she ignored, the number of times she had begged Jared Taylor to take some action in making the marriage better, all to no avail. Kate felt so utterly foolish because even when he refused, she stayed. There was no getting back to what they once had because there was really never anything there to begin with.

଻଼

Her husband's first affair started within the first week of their honeymoon trip to St. Barts. Kate was caught up in the sights and sounds of the place, the beauty and the culture that they were surrounded by. Jared Taylor had rented the Casa Del Mar for the entire month, and they were staying forever if she had anything to say about it. Every morning she would take walks outside, taking in the scenery, never wanting to forget how magical this place was. It was on one of those walks that her world turned upside down. She was on the deck overlooking the beach on the fourth day of their honeymoon smiling to herself. Everything had been perfect. The wedding was lavish, the reception beyond anything Kate could have dreamed, and her honeymoon...to say that Kate was glowing would be an understatement. She never had fantasies of Prince Charming growing up, and yet somehow she found herself in the middle of a fairy tale. It was on that day, overlooking the crystal blue water, she spotted a couple on the beach in the distance. She couldn't believe people actually *did* that type of thing in public. Even if there was no one around to see. Except for her. She saw. She decided she was embarrassed for them and started to turn away, but something caught her attention and she turned back to look again. The man had on a white button-down shirt, which was unbuttoned so far as she could tell, and he had sandy colored hair like Jared Taylor. She dismissed the similarities; *what man doesn't own a white dress shirt, after all?* She felt guilty for watching but continued to do so, until the phone rang. She looked for a caller ID and found no information.

"Hello?"

"Kate! You haven't called since you arrived! I was worried about you!"

Of ***course****, it's mom, calling me on my honeymoon while I watch two strangers on a beach practically mauling each other. Great. Freud would have a flippin' heyday over that kind of timing.* Kate was not too worried about thinking that thought out loud, she knew her mother would not have been paying much attention.

"Yes, we arrived here with no problems. It is so beautiful here mom, I wish I could work from here. Yes, I know it's unrealistic mom, but wow, we're *happy* here. I can't imagine a place I would rather be. Yes, mom, there's plenty of Catholic churches. No, mom, don't get your hopes up."

Jared Taylor walked in the door, covered in sand and wearing a wide grin.

"Mom, I'm going to have to let you go, Jared just walked in. Yes, mom, he's well. Yes, I'll tell him. Love you, too. Bye."

He grabbed Kate's waist as he stood behind her, and kissed the back of her neck.

"Jared, please! Let me hang up the phone at least!" Kate laughed and turned around to face him. Something was off, she noticed right away. He was all over her, which was not like him, even as a newlywed.

"Mom sends her love," she said, trying to shake the suspicion. She was embarrassed she would think such a thing, let alone ruin a romantic moment by mentioning her mother. "Sorry, Jared...I" she said, her eyes downcast.

"Nothing is going to ruin this, besides what man doesn't want to hear from his mother-in-law on his honeymoon?"

Jared laughed. "I would die a happy man if I could have this and you for the rest of my life," he said as lifted her chin up with his finger and kissed her.

Kate caught the faint scent of coconut on his lips. Her stomach flipped. The urge to ask him where he'd been, what he'd been doing and who he'd been with, was interrupted by the sound of her grandmother's voice in her head.

Better for a man to live on the corner of a roof than to share a house with a nagging wife.

Great, just what I want to hear on my honeymoon, Bible verses...gee, thanks, Gran, but if that ***was*** *him on the beach, the last thing he'd have to worry about is a roof; six feet under, maybe, but a roof? Naw.* Kate thought.

"What?" Jared Taylor said, wide-eyed,

She had said it out loud. Kate hesitated. The consequences of saying something to him about what she saw; could very well lead to an annulment. She knew Jared Taylor was not the type of man who dealt with confrontation well. She was well aware that he was competitive and ruthless in the business world, and she doubted if his approach toward his personal life was markedly different. Kate was not prepared to deal with the fallout of accusing her husband of an affair on their honeymoon. She loved it there too much. She loved *him* too much. Taking a deep breath and reaching for everything she had in her mental arsenal to fight the urge to scream, she smiled and changed the subject.

“Whatcha been trinkin' dis early, Islan Bouy?” she said in her feeble attempt at a Caribbean accent.

“Hey, we're on our honeymoon, there’s no law against a little rum in the morning now is there?” Jared Taylor answered, much to Kate's relief. The diversion worked. “I wish you could have joined me on the walk this morning, Kate. I just found the most romantic place for a campfire on the beach, I'll see if the concierge can set something up for us for tomorrow night. Hey, if you have time this afternoon, can you send my shirt to the cleaners? Blanchisserie Solaire is not too far from here, you know enough French to tell them not to put it on a hanger, don't you? If not, I'll just write it down, ummmm, I think the sticky notes are over there, on the desk. Oh, there's a button missing also, see if they'll fix that. I've got to shower and get over to the airport and get to St. Maarten for a round of golf with Pete.”

He was talking too fast, he was too happy, and that *shirt*. The pit in her stomach had opened up into a canyon, but she forced a smile.

“Oh, sure, I can. Why do you have to go to St. Maarten?”

“Sweetie, you know there's not a course on St. Barts! Pete flew all the way in from London last night, and I haven't seen him for years, I'll be back in the morning, you understand, don't you? I'll make it up to you, I promise."

Kate swallowed hard. "Yes, yes, of course. I'll find something to do. There's always shopping."

"Shopping, of course!" Jared Taylor laughed and got out his wallet. "I almost forgot to give this to you, it's yours, and your name is on it. Use it for whatever you want, whenever you want. I just want you to be happy."

Kate looked at the card that he had placed in her hand. A card with access to practically unlimited funds. She could put a down payment on a new house, fly to Europe, and bring the whole Brannigan clan along with her and barely make a dent in what was available to her financially. Her fingers slowly wrapped around the plastic, and she nodded to Jared Taylor, caressing the raised numbers on the front of the card back and forth. She was about to make a deal with herself that she would come to regret, but all she said was, "Thank you, sweetheart, have a good time golfing."

Kate never said a word about what she witnessed on the beach that day. She took his shirt to the cleaners and had the button re-sewn. She spent the rest of the honeymoon in a denial so deep that no one would have ever suspected that she had been betrayed. That ability to ignore her husband's affairs served its purpose for a very long time. She lived the life she had always dreamt of, aside from the adulterous husband part. If there was ever a conflict, some chance that she would not get what she wanted, Kate subtly hinted that she may have had some idea of what he was doing. It was the price she paid willingly until she changed her mind about everything. And then, of course, everything changed.

CHAPTER TEN

The bakery was warm, and the door, although still open, was propped to a smaller degree. "The heating bill just went up again, so I figured open halfway is better than all the way and certainly better than closed," Wally smiled.

"Wally, I was wondering if I could have your help with something..." Kate asked, licking the last bits of lemon filling from her fingertips.

"Sure Doc, what do you need?" Wally's face lit up at the request.

"I need some help finding a Christmas tree. I know it's not even Thanksgiving yet, but I want to make sure we have something special for Stella. Do you know where I would find a tree lot when the time comes?"

"I don't know where there is a tree lot, but I know where there's a LOT of TREES!!" Wally held one hand over his stomach and with his other hand, he slapped the counter as he laughed. He looked up at Kate, and when he realized she was not laughing, he cleared his throat and said, "Doc, there's acres of timber right behind your house, that's where you should get your tree."

"I know. You see, J.T. and Stella's father won't be able to make it this year, and so I'm kind of left to my own devices on this one. I'm dangerous with a butter knife, so I think pre-cut would be..."

"Nonsense!" Wally said. He put his hands on his hips and turned around to find the phone, his apron strings straining against his girth, as he bent over to grab a pen that had fallen on the floor. As he stood back up, he held his back and groaned. "Am not as young as I used to be, Doc. Might be hard to imagine now, but I was quite the catch when I was younger!" He winked and held his index finger up. "Not only that, I bake too!"

Kate laughed and started wiping the counter top with her napkin "Why didn't you ever marry?" she asked, surprising herself with such a personal question.

"Never had the time when I was younger, played some college ball in Missouri, moved back up here after my brother died, and spent a lot of years building up the business, such as it is."

"It's an incredible business, Wally. I'd bet with the right marketing you could be..."

"Nope. Already been approached," Wally interrupted as he shook his head. "There is something about trying to be bigger and better...most people spend a lot of time working toward it and wind up being neither. As for me, I like keeping it small. I like talking to people who aren't in too much of a hurry to get to the next best thing. Like you, Doc."

"Like *me?* You can't be serious. I am wound up tighter than a watch most of the time, and when I first met you I was so rude!" Kate waved him off and looked down at the bear claws and cinnamon rolls, breathing the aroma in as deeply as she could before exhaling and quickly inhaling again, pulling in her stomach while cinching the belt on her coat up tightly around her waist.

"Nah, Doc. You were just afraid, that's all. There's a difference."

"Me? Afraid? I'm a lot of things, but I've never been accused of being a coward." Kate bristled a bit, wondering where the Baker got *his* PhD.

"One day," Wally continued. "You'll come in here and say to yourself, "This. This is what I *really* want." But right now, you don't know, so you think if you spend enough time on the other side of that glass staring at all the pastries you'll figure it out. Not gonna figure it out by looking at 'em."

Kate started to interject, but the Baker continued.

"Not gonna figure it out by looking to see what everybody else is eating or not eating either. So instead you get mad, and you tighten your belt and deny yourself something so small. Such a pure pleasure, a donut. Could have been a loaf of bread, might have been a bagel., but somewhere the decision was made to change things just a little and it wound up a pastry, and that made it *bad,*" Wally shook his head.

Kate wanted to say something but felt guilty, as if she were in some sort of "Baker's church" listening to the sermon, so she let Wally continue.

"So go ahead and pull that belt in a little tighter to make you forget you're not satisfied. Nobody's saying you gotta eat chocolate éclairs every time you feel the urge, that's just dumb."

A look of deep sympathy washed over his face and he said earnestly, "It's okay Doc, if you really want it, to relax and let that belt out on your coat a little if you feel like a jelly donut now and then. It's no sin to exhale and let your stomach relax some, once in a while. Besides, I have it on good authority that confectioner's sugar is anti-aging.

"Really?!" Kate said, her interest renewed.

"Nah, just made that part up," Wally laughed. "Why settle for a kolach, as delicious as it is, when you really have your heart set on something chocolate covered with sprinkles on top."

"Sprinkles?" Kate laughed, half outraged by being psychoanalyzed by a man who spent most of the day covered in flour, and half amazed at how close to home he was hitting.

"Life's all about the sprinkles, sorry, once you get me going, I kind of get on a roll....get it...a *roll*!" Wally's eyes crinkled shut as he laughed at his own joke. He picked up the phone and walked into the kitchen, leaving Kate standing there alone. Leaving customers unsupervised was not something you did in L.A., and Kate wondered how many kids had stolen goodies from behind Mr. Jowalski's back over the years. She turned her back against the glass counter top and looked around.

One side looked as if it could double as a subway car, with bright orange benches facing the middle of the room and three metal poles standing floor to ceiling in front of them. She laughed at the thought of weary commuters munching on glazed donuts, going nowhere, looking listless and sipping coffee.

"Taken care of," Wally said, interrupting her daydream as he came out of the kitchen, leaving the swinging door open as he started up the fan that cooled the freshly baked bread, sending the smell outside into the cold Iowa afternoon.

"What's taken care of?" Kate asked, searching for her change purse.

"The Christmas Tree, silly! Someone from the Chamber of Commerce will be over after Thanksgiving with a

Welcome Basket and a saw. Your kids can go help pick the tree out if they like."

"Wally, I don't know what to say."

"Say yes." Wally's eyes twinkled.

"To sprinkles?" Kate laughed.

"To sprinkles!" Wally said as he held up a small, chocolate covered confection, tossed it into his mouth, wiped his hands off on his apron, grinned and winked at Kate. She started out the door then hesitated, waiting for Wally's goodbye.

"Thank you for visiting "Nice Buns!" Wally yelled as Kate stepped out into the cold, smiling.

On her way to the beauty shop, Kate hesitated, looked for a "perm in progress" sign and opened the door. Carla greeted her warmly and asked her if she was finding her way around okay.

"Well to be honest, as small as this town is, I still get myself turned around on occasion, and except for "Mighty Mart" and "Nice Buns" I haven't even ventured out to shop."

"Well, there's not much here, to be honest. These days we buy online, mostly," Carla said, rinsing a handful of brushes and combs as she spoke.

"There's a bunch of us that go to Chicago at least twice a year for a girls weekend, just after Thanksgiving and again right after Christmas to shop. We have come home with some fantastic deals, let me tell you. It is a blast! We shop, we talk, we drink, and eat...it would be wonderful if you could join us!" Carla said, as she worked a rinse into the scalp of an elderly lady who had remained motionless during the whole conversation.

Kate watched as Carla massaged the purple liquid in the sparse, gray hair that lay matted onto her head. She stared hard at the old woman's chest, trying to see if she could catch the rise and fall of her breath and saw nothing.

Stunned, she whispered the words "Is she...?" She looked straight at Em and spelled out, "D-E-A-D?" to Carla, looking horrified.

Suddenly the woman rose from the sink and shouted "NO! I'm not D-E-A-D!!! I'm not D-E-A-F either, SO CUT IT OUT!!!" She then shook her head and lay back down in the chair placing her neck into an exaggerated position, so that only Carla could see the roll of her eyes before she closed them again.

Carla glanced up in time to see Kate getting up off the floor, and dropping the rinse bottle in the sink behind the old woman's head, rushed to help her. "Up we go! There now, sit down, I'll get you some water."

"No, I'm okay....really, just startled," Kate waved her hand and nodded toward the woman that sat there staring at them both.

"Em, you really need to knock it off, you're about gonna go and give someone a darned heart attack!" Carla scolded.

"WHAT?" the woman lifted her head up looking confused.

Carla continued, shouting, "Em, this is Kate, the nice lady I was telling you about, you'll be talking to her next week."

"WHAT?" Em asked again.

Carla made her eyes wide and looked at Kate, shaking her head silently. Kate understood and waited, saying nothing for a few minutes before getting up and saying goodbye. "I have to get going Carla, but I will be back in on Monday. Pleased to meet you Em, I look forward to working with you. Have a good weekend, you two!"

Carla called out to her as she was leaving, "You have a good weekend too, Kate! Get back to me about Thanksgiving weekend, it would be fun! Oh! Have fun getting your first Iowa Christmas tree!"

Kate smiled and shook her head, *how in the world does news travel so fast around here*? "Thanks, Carla, the kids will be so thrilled! I can't wait to see the look on their faces when they find out they get to go out into the woods and hunt for their own!!"

"Oh, for goodness sake!" Em snapped, and sat up in her chair again and looked right at Kate. "I sure hope you are a better shrink than you are a farmer ya don't hunt for a Christmas tree, you go chop one down, they don't run away from ya for the love of Pete!!

"Of course, that is what I meant, and you are absolutely right, ma'am, I am not a farmer, I'm from California, thank you for your patience while I acclimate." Although Kate's voice sounded sincere, her face was contorted from trying to hold in her laughter. "Good-bye, I'll get back to you about Chicago, Carla—and nice meeting you, Em!" she yelled before walking out the door. The thought of going somewhere with a bunch of women she hardly knew to go shopping somewhere hours away was actually very comforting, of all the things she had experienced so far, it was the first thing that she was familiar with.

CHAPTER ELEVEN

If it had not had been for the scare with Em, Kate might not have sensed that someone was watching her as she headed to her car. Her adrenaline was still coursing and she was back to the same state of hyper vigilance that she had become accustomed to in the city.

"I know a body shop that can get this ding out for less than $75.00 if you tell them you are a friend of mine."

The voice wasn't familiar, it was much deeper than she would have imagined his to be, but she knew who it was. Sawyer. He was leaning against the hood of her car, with one lanky leg resting in front of the other one. Kate froze in her tracks, looked straight at him, then dropped to her knees and started furiously digging through her purse.

"Ugh! Why can't I just find the...." Kate's hands were clawing through her belongings like the crane in the game she used to play at the State Fair as a child. Not finding what she was looking for, she took her hands from her purse and rested them on her knees "Just so you know, I have..."

Sawyer held out his hand "I always carry a small can of mace with me if that's what you are looking for. Here, you take it."

She glared at him for a moment, trying to think of something to say, then grabbed her purse, turned it upside down and shook the entire contents onto the ice-patched sidewalk. She sat down in the snow and proceeded to rummage through the spill and still not finding what she was looking for, started scraping it all back up, including the bits of dirty snow and wet paper, then stood up and brushed the snow off of her backside.

"Just who do you think you *are*?!" Kate screamed at the top of her lungs, her arms rigid and glued to her sides.

"Calm down now, I may be as harmless as a housefly, but I don't appreciate being yelled at," Sawyer said as he put the container of WD-40 back in his pocket.

"Annnd three strikes! Yerrrrrr Out!" she whispered under her breath. It was his *voice*. Her whole demeanor changed as soon as she heard it again. It acted as a verbal form of kryptonite, causing Kate to feel oddly powerless to stay angry.

"I, I, I am so sorry Mr. Sawyer?" Kate's attempt at being offended had just vaporized.

"Ma'am." Sawyer nodded his head and moved to the driver's side door of her car.

"Thank you, umm..." Kate could not form a sentence. She decided that the move was indeed an act of chivalry and not a well-mannered attempt at a car-jacking. Her mind was racing, her head hurt, and she realized that any attempt at saving face was completely lost, so she stopped trying to think of something to say and just got into her car.

She looked up as he was closing the door and watched him shake his head. "Take it easy on the way home, you can just pull straight ahead from here, so you'll be okay," he laughed as he motioned to her mirror then turned around and walked toward the bakery. Kate just smiled knowing that any thought she may have said out loud by accident would have been safely drowned out by the car stereo.

CHAPTER TWELVE

The news was not good. The first draft of the divorce papers had arrived. Kate grumbled to herself as she searched for her reading glasses, *what had happened to waiting a year?* She read something about a Trust and the words "In lieu of" and "continuing the community garden, to ensure the Swifton family legacy of commitment toward self-sufficiency, and the ability to blah, blah, blah. Katherine Brannigan shall henceforth be responsible for the payment of all taxes, and insurance and blah, blah, blah."

"That son-of-a," was the best Kate could come up with as she sat down at the kitchen table, coffee cup half empty and her mind completely full. She was not sure what those words meant, exactly, but she knew it couldn't be good. If Jared Taylor was trying to get to her, it worked. She felt off balance and angry. *She* was the one who was betrayed, *she* was the one who was lied to all those years, and yet *she* was expected to agree to a bunch of *In Lieu of's* just because he had the money to make it happen?

Kate knew she was no saint, but the thought of all the times she had swallowed her pride for the sake of keeping everything together, made her angry. *Did I not try to be amiable? Did I not try to smile and nod appreciatively when Jared Taylor's mother would offer unsolicited advice? And didn't I hold my tongue when I wanted to say, "While we're on the subject of how to raise children, Margaret, why, exactly, would I want my kids to turn out like the man I am divorcing?"*

So ya made yer' own bed---so what? Doesn't mean ya have to lie in it forever, darlin'. Kate imagined what Maeve would tell her.

Jared Taylor's voice also made its way into her head. *Kate, you are overly dramatic, quit getting so wound up about everything, or you can just stay there and enjoy the land of milk and manure.* He always managed to stay so calm when he insulted her. It drove Kate crazy.

He could tell her she was simply too unintelligent without sounding like he was cruel, which was actually crueler, in Kate's opinion. "*Why work, when you are so much better suited to a lifestyle of looking beautiful and being quiet?*" would come out in the exact same tone of voice as he would use to say, "*Good morning, sweetheart,*" while perusing the financial section of the morning paper.

Kate's stomach knotted. Between the letter from Jared Taylor and the thought of actually having to use the repair shop recommended by Sawyer before Jared Taylor could find out about her mirror error, panic set in. She threw the letter in her purse and headed into town. Half-way there, she realized that she didn't have the directions to the shop. After pulling over to have a cry before she went any further, she decided that she would skip her regular stop into the bakery as the thought of a pastry on top of the sinking feeling she had in the pit of her stomach did not seem like a good idea. Besides, she was mad, and Wally would only try and cheer her up. She was not in the mood for a sermon, no matter how sweet.

Maeve. *She* would understand. The only one in the whole town that Kate felt may actually have been a little more of a mess than herself. They had spent a couple of hours together nearly every day since they first met, Maeve taking on the role of "Town Ambassador", introducing her to folks and giving Kate the background information on the businesses and families that made up the community.

Having a real friend was something of a new experience for Kate. Even in college, she didn't get too close to anyone. It wasn't that she disliked people, she just always put friendship in the same category as she did shoes. They got her where she wanted to go, but were generally too much of a pain to have to be in all the time, and if they didn't make you look good, they were not worth keeping around.

The smell of cigarette smoke escaping from the window beside the office door told Kate that Maeve was there, so she came in, expecting a great big hug and stories to distract her. Instead, she was caught off guard by the redhead who appeared before her. Maeve was sitting at her desk with a scowl on her face, drumming her fleshy fingers on the desk. Kate thought she looked like a female version of an Irish Don Corleone, and it made her smile to picture her friend making someone *an offer they can't refuse*.

“Been expecting you, Kate, we need to talk,” Maeve said.

“Oh, I know! Wait a minute, you were expecting me?” Kate, still breathless from the cold air and her quick step, was too caught up in the contents of the letter she had received, and started in on the audacity of him expecting so much and how dare *he* do that to *her.* After a long diatribe about the roles of women in patriarchal society and the evil corporate agenda, she slumped up against the wall and shook her head.

“I don't think there is one good man left in this world, I swear, Maeve, I feel blindsided completely.”

“Are you quite done?” Maeve asked, and not giving Kate a moment to answer, launched in, “*You* wouldn't know a good man from a Snickers Bar, Kate Brannigan. In fact, by the looks of you, you haven't had one of those for a while either, so let's just say you are missing out on two of the most important things in life. Men and chocolate. Chocolate and men. Oh, and beer.” Maeve's voice trailed and she looked caught up in thought. Kate started to clear her throat but Maeve held her hand up, “Now obviously I know a little more about chocolate and beer, but that's beside the point.

Maeve stood up and pressed her fingertips into her desk continuing, “You march in, ranting on with the “How dare he" bit. Well, how dare *you,* how about that? Where do you get off slinging insults and getting all self-righteous when one of the truest, kindest men I have ever known, just tries to help you? Sawyer was just being a gentleman, just attempting to be nice to you and you freak out on him like that? My *God* I just don't *get* you, Kate. I know we haven't known each other long, but from what I see, it's as if you are the dictator of your own little country sitting in constant fear of a coup d'état and yet, you are the sole inhabitant."

"Well. Thank you for your honesty, Maeve, sincerely," Kate said sarcastically. What is with all you people trying to analyze *me*? I'm the psychologist, for crying out loud! Tell me, do you even know what coup d'état means? Or did you rehearse that one just in case you could use it some day?" For the first time, Kate noticed just how condescending her voice could sound, and she looked down.

Maeve's lips quivered just slightly and she looked up at the ceiling before staring straight at Kate. "I know we seem like we're a bunch of backward dolts to you, but get this straight, Miss Sacramento, L.A. or Los *wherever,* we are not phony. You are. Just look at you. So quick to judge people you know so very little about."

"We know why you are here, and we *know* how you feel about us," Maeve continued with the tempo that did not allow for any interruption, "and we are kind anyway. But don't think for one minute that you can go around taking out your anger on *my* friends. If you think you can go around acting like a rabid dog, taking out all the rage that you feel toward your husband and turning it around on Sawyer, don't think for a minute you aren't going to get an earful." Before Kate could raise her hand in protest, Maeve added, "I think in your line of work, they call it *Displacement,* but hey, what would I know? You're the *psychologist*, after all."

In the time it took for her to finish her lecture, she had walked around her desk and met Kate at the front entrance across from the steps that led to the attic. She sat down on one of them in a giant heap, her red hair flying across her forehead, sticking to the sweat that had started to bead up and run down her face, mixing with a few tears before pooling on the ledge atop her fleshy cheeks.

Kate tried to draw in a breath, but she could not. The blood had rushed to her face and all she wanted to do was disappear. She sank to the floor, looked up at Maeve, and just stared. Her shoulders and head started to shake in unison as if dancing to a silent song. Then it happened. A cry escaped Kate's mouth and she made no effort to contain it She could not have pinched her cheeks hard or fast enough to stop what was happening. She started shouting incoherently, pounding her fists on her knees. She stopped suddenly when she felt the thick arms of her temporary adversary wrap around her, it startled her. She looked up into Maeve's eyes, frightened. *What had just happened here? What in the world?*

"Alright now, there, there." Maeve cooed as if she were soothing a baby. For the first time, Kate detected the slight brogue in her voice as she rocked her back and forth.

"How 'bout you and I go out for a pitcher of Coors at Kandy Lanes? We could grab a beer, bowl a little?" she unwrapped her arms and got up suddenly, leaving Kate to drop to one elbow.

"What? Is this for real or am I dreaming all this up?"

Maeve helped her to her feet and said, "You know what they say, don't you? That to be best friends, you have to have at least one major fight and we just had ours. Best to get it out of the way now. C'mon now let's go have a pint to *celebrate.*

Before Kate could utter a word in protest, Maeve held up her hand. "Carla will watch the kids, she's got two of her own, ya know, it'll be a big slumber party. Now come on, let's go."

CHAPTER THIRTEEN

Kate did not generally play with fire. However, her mouth felt as if she had been drinking it straight out of the bottle. "The bowling alley is such a bowling alley, why have I never been to one before? This is so very reeeeeel! It is very, very, "bowling-alley-ee!" she was later rumored to have said, but in Kate's mind, if she didn't remember it, then it didn't happen. That was a stance that she questioned when she woke up the next morning in the same clothes she wore the night before and questioned even more so when she reached for the screaming alarm clock and found a pack of cigarettes alongside a book of matches with Sawyer's name and number inside. She sat straight up in bed at the sight of it and immediately fell back onto the pillow holding her head with both hands.

Maeve's voice came up through the floor register "Up and at 'em, Madam! Breakfast is ready!!" Kate leaned over the bed to look down through it, remembering that as a child, she and her cousins would play detectives and peer down through the cast iron floor vent in her grandmother's bedroom to spy on the adults below. They would listen in on conversations that took place around the dining room table over a game of cards or after dinner drinks. That was how she found out that her brother was flunking algebra, that the quiet neighbor lady was caught shoplifting, and that her uncle was going back to college. It was also how, peering through that grate, she learned that her grandmother was diagnosed with lung cancer. That was the last conversation that she ever eavesdropped on through that grate. There was no coming back downstairs pretending she didn't hear what was just said, after something like that.

Kate slowly got up and found her way to the top of the stairs, noticing the row of pictures that hung on the wall as she headed down. The house was quiet and tidy, but too formal for someone like Maeve. It was too lacy, too dark, too *old.* Not that she was picturing a neon beer light in the window or a poster of *Celtic Thunde*r over her bed, but this house was not Maeve's. This house very definitely belonged to Maeve's father.

"Dad's visiting his sister, he won't be back until the day after tomorrow, so cheers!" Maeve held up a glass of red juice in the air like a disheveled statue of liberty.

"Bring me your poor, your downtrodden, your huddled forty-something divorcees," Kate said, raising her own glass. At that moment, Maeve reminded her of a high school girl having a party while the parents were out of town.

"Everyone in town has to know about this already, maybe I should just wait and ask them what happened." Kate quipped. "You know," she continued, looking into her glass, “you’re going to turn me into a lush, Maeve. What the heck is in this?”

“It's best if you don't know, but you feel better now don't cha? I like to call it my V-GRREEAT!” Maeve yelled, in an overly exaggerated thick brogue that reminded Kate of an Irish version of “Tony the Tiger.”

She prepared herself for the worst when she remembered that the children were with Carla. “The kids! What was I thinking, I have to get home!” she said as she attempted to lift herself from the kitchen chair and run out the door, but her legs were lead and she couldn't quite manage to stand up from the seated position. Maeve reassured her that the children were fine, and had quite a wonderful time at their very first slumber party with Carla's children.

Kate felt horrible that she never asked any of the women that she'd met with about their families or what their lives were like. She didn't even ask about how she wound up at Maeve's house at first, mostly because she was not sure she wanted to hear the answer. By the time she had finished a couple of glasses of the drink, however, she was ready to ask about the evening before, bracing herself.

She felt the tightness in her hands relax as she was informed that no, she had not started smoking again. The cigarettes she woke up to were Maeve's, and the number on the book of matches was Sawyer's. Kate had asked for his number, but that it was only so that he could seal the pantry drawer shut permanently, as she didn't want to leave it open for security purposes.

"I actually *said* that? *Security purposes*? Those were my exact words?" Kate could not believe her ears. *What a piss poor excuse to get a phone number.* She looked up at Maeve immediately to make sure that *that particular thought* stayed in her head, where it belonged.

The "V-Great" was starting to settle in her stomach creating a warmth that she could only describe as comforting. That made her feel uneasy, so she raised her hand and shook her head when Maeve started to pour another. "I have to get something to eat or I'll never make it out of this house, Mr. Jawolski would be proud at this "loosening the belt a little" moment," she mused.

"Shoot!" Maeve exclaimed.

"What?"

"Mr. Jawolski! The Kolach Festival! We're all supposed to be meeting at the bakery to plan the trip up to St. Ludmila's in June, for the festival...shoot!" Maeve put down her glass and stood up, suddenly sober.

"How do you dooooo that?" Kate said, feeling the full effects of the drink rushing to her head. "How do you just get un-drunk like that?" she tried to snap her fingers, and after a few futile attempts waved her hand and continued, "What about St. Ludmila? What about kolaches? Tell me, I'm a therapist, I understand. Did you have something bad happen to you and you find yourself overeating to compensa---" she stopped short. She had been talking to herself, Maeve had disappeared. Kate looked at her fingers quizzically and tried snapping them again, and waited for her to re-appear.

"C'mon, let's get going! We are sooooo late!"

Maeve came flying around the hallway corner, as Kate stared at her newly discovered magical snapping fingers in utter amazement. Maeve started to grab Kate's arm, then let go and lifted her off the chair, setting her down in front of the door.

"Here are your things, now let's go!"

"You need a planning committee to go eat donuts?" Kate slurred, as she poured into the back seat of Kate's car.

"Don't ever call them *donuts* in front of Mr. Jawolski, he'd throw a fit! I'm sorry you gotta sit back there, my front seat's a mess and we have to get a move on, I can't believe how late I am!"

Kate was drunk. However, she was not so drunk that she didn't catch on that Maeve was getting a little more flustered than the situation called for.

"What's wrong, Maeve? Wally won't be upset, he's not like that, he'll understand."

"Well, now. You haven't been in town a month, and you already have a nickname for our Baker," Maeve said, visibly upset.

"What? I? No. NO." Kate tried hard not to slur, "I didn't make up a nickname! HE told me to call him that."

"Oh. Is that so? Even better. Humph." Maeve quipped. Only her eyes were visible in the rear view mirror, but Kate was getting the definite sense that the meeting was a *lot* more important to Maeve that it was to anyone else.

"Maeve?"

"Yah?" Maeve said looked into the mirror to see Kate fumbling in her purse.

"What do you think of Mr. Jawolski?" "I mean, he's a nice man, never married, and from what he tells me, he's been here a long time and not leaving here anytime soon, did you ever think...."

"*THINKING*!" Maeve interrupted, "*thinking* is what gets people into messes all the bah-LESS-ed time. *Thinking* got you hitched to the wrong man. *Thinking* made me stay here to take care of my dad instead of asking him what HE wanted to do. *Thinking* got us both to where we are, so thank you very much if I don't tell you what I THINK." The blinkers indicated a left-hand turn, but Maeve pulled off to the right and shifted the car into park.

Maeve turned to Kate, her thick hands pinching the upholstery at the top of the bench seat, serving as an anchor to keep her there. "SO. What words of wisdom are you gonna throw at me now Kate? What would "Dr. Brannigan," say?" Maeve said, looking directly at her.

"What I would say is not the same thing as what I would do, or have done for that matter." Kate stopped searching through her bag and ran her fingertips up and down the small metal clasp that kept the contents shut. "See this purse?" she continued. "This purse has my life in it, from lipstick and cell phone to photos and credit cards." She stopped.

Maeve looked at her for a moment and said, "Annnnd?"

"Annnd, that's all you get for 5 minutes, I charge $200.00 an hour Maeve, and I figure I drank about $25.00 worth of your liquor and I'll deduct cab fare because I think you are taking me somewhere. You are taking me somewhere, aren't you Maeveeeee?"

"What in the blue blazes are you even talking about?" Maeve bellowed, releasing her grip on the seat, which caused her to spring forward and face the road in front of them. She began to shift the car back into drive when Kate started to laugh.

"No, stop! I was just kidding! Seriously, Maeve! I was joking, I'll tell you what I think, and honestly it's the first real original thought of mine I've had for years, actually, uh, never mind."

Suddenly, Kate felt dizzy and nauseous and was grateful the car was parked as she lunged forward to open the door, screaming "I'm gonna be sick! C'mon and help me get this seat up so I can get out!" The contents of the "V-Great" landed directly on the front windshield and dash, miraculously pooling and running into the coffee mug that was nestled in the cup holder on the dashboard.

"Well, this is fun now, isn't Doctor? Or should I call you Kate? Perhaps I should call you Ms. Brannigan, or was it still Mrs. Swifton? See, it would be nice to know which one of you I am talking to because it's obvious one of you has no capacity to hold her liquor, and she's the one I'd like to finish cleaning up this bloody mess!

Maeve was sweating and furiously trying to catch the remains of the morning and guide it into the mug, while Kate sat in the passenger seat, on top of books and papers and half-smoked cigarettes, trying not to vomit anymore.

"What do you mean, 'which one of you'? I don't get it. I am the one talking right?" Kate asked, trying to breathe in the cold air and mentally force the nausea to subside.

"I mean, you present yourself one way to people if it suits you, and another way if it suits you better," Maeve started, "wait a minute, you have no idea that you do that do you? How could you? You are so busy running from yourself that you don't even have a clue. Tell you what, *Doc*, why don't you try fixing *yourself* before you start taking in any patients. Now get in, I don't have time for this, we're late and we're going. I'll drop you off at your office and you can clean up there, and here's a thought, why don't you lie down on that nice couch we just took from Doc Martin's things and think about helping whoever you are at the moment." Maeve was not making a suggestion, it was an order, and Kate complied.

CHAPTER FOURTEEN

The bathroom heat in the office had not been turned up and Kate was freezing. "I'm spending way too much time in front of sinks these days," she said as she splashed the cool water on her face. Still a bit drunk, she tried unsuccessfully to bend her head in such a way that it would allow her to fit it underneath the spigot so that she could rinse her hair out but the sink was too shallow, and she found herself caught between its sides and the hot water faucet. After banging her head against the porcelain trying to break free, she tried a different angle, and then another. Nothing was working, so she gave up. As she stood up, she caught her reflection in the mirror and gasped. The woman staring back at her was unrecognizable. Kate touched the mirror and let her fingers glide down the smooth glass, stopping at the point where her fingers met the reflection of where her heart was.

"*The righteous cry, and the Lord Heareth and delivereth them out of all their troubles.* Her grandmother's voice echoed in her head.

"Again with the Bible quotes, Gran?" Kate said. "Okay, let's try it your way. I don't know how "righteous" I am but whatever...I'm drunk enough to give it a whirl.

"Hey!" Kate said looking up, trying not to lose her balance as she did so. "Whoever! Can't you see I need some help?" Her slurred words got louder and faster. "Why do I have to ask like a groveling child? *Why* do I have to beg you?" Kate stared up at the water stained ceiling and yelled "DO SOMETHING? Oh, that's right. You don't like me, that's it. Well, so sorry. Hey, why would I even want to believe in You anyway?! Yeah, You hear me?"

Kate paused then looked up "I'm listening...hello? You there? *Whatever.* I don't need any God who plays games like this!" Kate hesitated, the thought of a newspaper headline saying, "*Charred Remains of New Psychologist Found in Dr. Bauer's Building, Freak Lightning Strike to Blame*" crossed her mind and she fell to the couch.

"Okay, You win, I'm asking. I'm *asking*. Just go ahead, wave your magic wand and fix this. Please? I'm going to go pass out now, do me a favor? Wake me up when You are done fixing my life."

CHAPTER FIFTEEN

Maeve walked into the bakery still disheveled and smelling like baby wipes and tomato juice. She found her way to the closest chair to the door and was hit by the aroma of baking bread. Immediately she calmed down, primped a bit and tried to pay attention to what was being said.

"So, we have the bus reserved. It seats fifty-six comfortably, and since it looks like there are only thirty-five of us going this year, we'll have plenty of room." Wally announced, his baritone voice booming without the aid of a loudspeaker.

"I thought we had thirty-seven?" came a voice from the crowd.

"Nope, it's thirty-five, Ester Smith passed on two Thursdays ago now, and, of course, Sawyer's wife, well...." Wally's eyes searched the room for Sawyer, and finding him nodded his head and continued, "She's going to be attending in spirit, if she's not up to dealing with the likes of us, but I'm sure Sawyer will be able to talk her into coming. So, if there is nothing else, let's wrap it up...I've got some hot buns that need tending too," Wally winked at Maeve and she felt the heat rising to her cheeks. "Don't blush, Maeve, don't blush," she whispered as she looked down, smiling.

CHAPTER SIXTEEN

Kate awoke to a knock on her office door. It was Carla, who called out from the other side of the only thing that was keeping the real world away for a while, and the real world was the very last thing that Kate was prepared to deal with. She glanced at the clock, it was only eleven in the morning, and although she had only been sleeping for a couple of hours, she felt as if I had been days. "Just a second!" she called out as cheerfully as she could. She stood up and looked still feeling a little queasy but she managed to walk over to the door and open it. Carla smiled and stared at Kate a moment, then looked past her, into the office, and back at her as if she were waiting for an invitation to sit down and talk. Although it was positively the last thing that she wanted to do, Kate smiled nervously, stood back from the door and invited her in. Carla gave her a hug and started in on a one-sided conversation; because the pounding in Kate's head prevented her from doing anything more than smile and nod. Carla said that she had stopped by to check and see if Kate was okay, if there was anything she could do.

"The kids got off to school just fine, and I can pick them up from school too if you need me to, and oh, here's a coffee. It was the V-Great's, wasn't it? I warned Maeve to go easy on you...I'm sorry you don't feel well, hon. Is there anything I can do?"

If she were even remotely religious, Kate would have sworn she saw a halo of light hovering around this woman. She decided it was still the booze and waved her away.

"No, I've got it. Thank you so much, Carla, you really are an angel. I've got my first appointment at ten this morning with Em so I will tell you what you *can* do for me, you can wish me luck!"

Carla laughed as she walked out the door, "Sure thing! You know what Miss Kate? We are all glad you are here, just wanted you to know that."

Kate didn't believe in a lot, but she could find comfort in the genuine spirit of people like Carla, who owed her nothing and didn't want anything from her, she was just decent. "I really could get used to this," she sighed as she sipped her coffee and prepared her notes for her appointment with Em.

ଓଃ

The metronome sounded quietly in the corner, and Kate's pencil was tapping on her teeth in time with it.

"I don't get it, you get paid $200.00 an hour to just sit there and watch me breathe? You could be doing that while I get my hair done!" Em said.

"No, I get paid to help you through what it is that's bothering you, and you and I work together to find a solution," Kate laughed.

"There is no solution to my problem," Em quipped.

"Oh, come on now, let's try, shall we? What is the problem?"

"I miss my husband. He left me four years ago," Em whispered.

Kate felt panic set in, not sure exactly how to proceed. All of the schooling, the clinical practicum, the training, all of it… flew out the window. She knew how to treat any problem on paper. How, though, did she ever think that she was ready to do this in real life?

"Well, I see. Divorce is not unheard of as one enters their golden years, people grow apart..."

"You're an idiot!" Em sat straight up from the couch she was lying on and looked straight at Kate. "My husband *died*! We didn't *divorce*! I knew I shouldn't have come here!"

Kate gulped, and held her hand out "No, Em, I'm sorry, I just thought since you said he left you, please, lay back down. Do you want some water?"

"No. He *did* leave me. He's gone and I'm here all alone, and I'm pissed off! There. You happy now?" Em looked at

Kate and shook her head. "I *told* Carla that you didn't know your ass from a hole in the ground!!"

Kate sat speechless, watching Em attempt to grab her walker handles.

"Little help here?" Em finally shouted.

"No. I mean, yes I will help you out, but you are right you are *so* right, Em, I don't know my ass from a hole in the ground," Kate smiled. Then Em turned to her, the skin around her eyes crinkling behind a broad smile "Well, there we go. Now *that's* progress. I'll be back same time next week?"

As Kate watched Em get up, this time with no need for assistance whatsoever, she noticed that the hand that she favored was her left. "You need to be able to express yourself through your art more confidently," she heard herself say.

Em turned suddenly, "What?!"

"Cripes, I am so sorry, this has been a disaster, Em... don't worry, I won't charge you. That was my inside voice," Kate chastised herself and shook her head, afraid to look up.

"Who told you?!" Em insisted.

"Told me what?"

"Told you that I painted?! Who told you?" Em turned from the direction of the office door straight toward Kate.

"No one told me anything, Em. I promise. I just noticed that..."

"Well, I suppose you are right. I have put it down long enough. He's not coming back so I can start again. He always hated me painting," Em said as she sat back down on the couch, and reached for a tissue and looked down.

Kate did not notice any tears, but she felt as if she had to do something. She went from wanting to touch Em's hand, to being terrified of it. The skin was crepey and so thin, that the blue veins just below the surface were clearly visible, pulsing rhythmically. She didn't know if she was helping or making it worse by staying silent. Finally, she pulled her chair a bit closer to the couch.

"I am sorry that your husband did not appreciate your art, that doesn't mean you can't do it now, for yourself," Kate rested her elbows on her knees, leaning in a little.

"What are you talking about? I never said he hated my paintings, I said he hated me *painting*...he hated the smell. He was worried about all the chemicals I was inhaling, he worried about me...always worried about me. Now he's the one that's dead and I am still here. He did appreciate my art, he just didn't like the process...it's just like marriage.

"Say again?" Kate asked, dazed, still trying to figure out where, exactly, she had misunderstood Em.

"I said, kind of like marriage, you know, we like the end result, we like to *say* we are married, we like the idea of it. The process smells like paint thinner mixed with Lava Soap and it makes you sick sometimes. No one likes the work," Em sighed. "Next week, Doc, I'll bring a couple in to show you."

By the time Kate looked up, Em was gone.

CHAPTER SEVENTEEN

The sign read: "Sometimes the only thing you can count on is that fact that you can't count on anything but the only thing, God's Love. Inquire inside."

Kate looked at the letter board outside of the little brick church that sat just outside the city limits to the east. She could hardly think of a time when city limits meant anything to her; all of the suburbs had blended together without seams where she was from, the only thing dividing most of the Greater Los Angeles area were freeways and off-ramps. She hadn't had to complain about taking the 405 and how long she was stuck in traffic, here. Kate had, in fact, spent some time figuring out just how many hours a day she had gained by moving to a two lane town with six side streets, and the total came to just about enough time to realize how much of a mess she'd become. The extra hours went quickly at first. She spent a lot of her time unpacking and repacking the things that weren't hers but Jared Taylor's that she had taken by mistake. Not that he would ever have missed any of it, not that anything couldn't be replaced, and not that he didn't have enough of that money to replace anything that needed replacing, including her. That thought stuck in her gut and churned around inside of her until she tasted bitter bile in her mouth. She felt sick. Why couldn't she get past that? She knew he'd had affairs before, why did this one bother her so much?

Perhaps it was the fact that while she was fighting aging, he was looking more handsome than ever. Kate felt like the short end of a long stick and it made her angry. It was more than just unfair, it was cruel. They had been married almost 14 years, and she didn't even know what he really did for a living. She thought it had something to do with securities, but he might as well have been a used car salesman for all she cared. She just knew that since the St. Barts incident, the credit card she carried was always paid in full. If she wanted to go off with her girlfriends for a week to Cancun she had a nanny and the means to go.

She had more options than she knew what to do with, and she was desperately unhappy about it. She wanted someone to tell her "no." "No, you can't stay home while I go to Italy because I'll miss you too much if you do. No, you don't get to buy the Prius, and I don't care about the carbon footprint, you have a perfectly good car right now," or most of all, "No, I don't love *anyone* more than I love you." She never heard that. "If you don't know by now how I feel, then it makes me question if I should feel the way I do," he told her once. She sat silently, trying to think of something to say back to him, to convince him his thinking was wrong. Kate said nothing. The most in-depth communication they were capable of came after the evening nightcaps when they would either tangle up with each other in bed or get into a tangle outside of it.

To the outside world, everything was spit shined and buttoned up. Everything was okay and she hated "okay", it was one of those debatable words that begged investigation. "Good-okay, okay-okay, or bad okay." It was more than that, though. He never really knew who she was or seemed to care, for that matter. *How can you know someone who doesn't know herself, though, really*? If she had been her own patient the solution to her distress would have been to write a prescription for an anti-depressant, perhaps another for anxiety, book a follow-up therapy session and send herself on her way. The thing was, there was no pill, and there was no magic potion to help her right now. Modern medicine had yet to come up with a cure for "stuck trying to figure out what in the world to do."

She got out of the car and went inside the little church, which was as nondescript as it was non-denominational. Kate was used to ornate statues, stained glass, and marble. This place could just as easily have been a high school cafeteria. She felt very out of place and a little sad. Somehow she thought that if she just came in and sat down that she would feel entirely different.

A man in a brown business suit came walking in from one of the side doors in the front of the room. He noticed Kate and smiled warmly, "Why you must be the famous "Dr. Brannigan, welcome!" Kate was taken aback, how could he know who she was?

"Why yes, and you are?" Kate said as she stood up and extended her hand.

“I'm Robert Williams, but everybody around here just calls me Pastor Bob,” he said as he smiled and shook her hand.

“Nice to meet you, Mr. Williams, everyone around here calls me Kate,” she said, looking to see if the failure to address him as “pastor” would get a reaction, she was relieved when he didn't seem to notice.

“Kate, so glad to meet you, here, sit down. To what do we owe the pleasure of your company today?”

“*We?*” Kate asked, looking around to see who else had shown up.

“Yes, well, it’s just me, actually, but I happen to think God’s here too,” the man's smile broadened.

“Oh, my...I'm sorry, I didn't come in here to convert or anything, I'm Catholic. I just thought I'd check this place out.” Kate felt a surge of guilt for using the “I'm Catholic” card, considering she hadn't been to Mass in years.

“Don't worry, I'm glad you came by.”

“*You* are glad; does that mean God's not so hot with the idea of me popping in?” Kate smiled.

The pastor continued to smile, but he looked at Kate curiously. “I think it's safe to say He's pretty thrilled with the idea, actually.”

Kate laughed, and then looked over at the simple wooden cross that hung on the wall in front of her, “I really don't know why I'm here, just wanted to see if...” Kate paused and looked down, then continued, “Honestly, I have nothing to complain about, I mean, I've *never* been exactly happy, but didn't realize *how* not exactly happ*y,* until I moved here…does that make sense?”

“Of course, it does, Kate, and from what I have heard, you have been through a lot.” The pastor leaned over and touched the top of the pew in front of him.

“Who the hel—lllo... I'm in a *church*, definitely *not* supposed to swear in a church, right? Okay...”

“Who in the world.” the pastor offered.

“What?”

“Who in the *world*, you could say that instead.”

“Have you read the *news*, lately, Pastor? Believe me, it's the *same* word.” Kate said sarcastically. Look, I'm so sorry, tell God I'm sorry too, I really should go.

The pastor stood up too, but his demeanor had changed. “If you want to apologize to God, you're going to have to tell Him that yourself, but don't ever feel like you have to apologize to *me*. Is it okay if I ask why you *really* came in here today?”

“What if I told you, I have no earthly idea why?” Kate replied.

“Then I would have to tell you that there's not a lot I can do, I'm sorry,” Pastor Williams said.

Kate took a deep breath and rolled her eyes. “Okay. Here's the thing, the real reason I am here. For the last few months, I've been hearing my dead grandmother's voice, prattling on about one Bible verse or another, and I think I may be going crazy. It's not the first time I've ever heard her voice, but it's happening a lot more often. I figured I'd stop in here first to see if there were any better answers before checking myself in over at Bellevue,” she meant to deliver that thought with dripping sarcasm, but it came out sounding more than a little desperate.

“You are the psychologist, Ms. Brannigan, you more than I would be able to tell if you need to go to a mental hospital.”

“I'm not schizophrenic if that's what you're aiming at.”

“Well, then consider an alternate answer. Use your reasoning skills. You know that what you are hearing is not actually your grandmother. Memories of her, perhaps, but not *her.* Maybe you recall certain things she used to say as a way to provide you with a way to cope, a way to make sense, a sense of direction.”

“Does that mean I have to start coming to church? Because I can tell you right now, I am *not* ready for *that*.”

"What is it you are looking for, exactly, Kate?"

"Faith in *something*, I suppose," Kate said, "I thought I would always have faith in my husband when we married. I thought I would always have faith in myself. I always believed that I could just figure everything out, you know? Everything I planned fell into place so perfectly and wound up so horrid. I can't figure out what I did wrong."

The pastor looked at Kate and nodded his head. Then he smiled, "Maybe you didn't do *anything* wrong. In fact, since you are here, from where I am sitting, you did everything exactly *right,* because it all led you to here. Don't you see? Faith isn't always acquired in one fell swoop. Sometimes faith trickles through the cracks in a heart that has hardened, until it softens up a little, sometimes it takes time."

"I just always thought that…I mean, what some people in your line of work have told me, is that, I am going to burn for all eternity, unless, of course, I go to *their* church, give *them* money, act like *they* act, believe everything *they* interpret, without hesitation. Look, I'm afraid I could never be like that. I'm impatient, I swear once in a while, I like a glass of wine or two..."

"Look, Ms. Brannigan, I think God will meet you right where you are. You can't earn His love, it's already there. How about this...just take it slowly, but do one thing different, take a look at the world as if God does exist, instead of assuming He doesn't. Try it for a while, see if you notice anything changing in your life, then come back and we'll chat."

"I guess I can't see any harm in that, although I will have to tell you, don't get your hopes up," Kate said, as she threw the strap of her purse over her shoulder and stood up .

"Sounds like you just might be getting closer to what you really want than you think. We'll talk soon...it was nice to meet you, Katherine Brannigan," the pastor smiled and shook Kate's hand, then stood up and walked Kate to the door.

CHAPTER EIGHTEEN

It was only a matter of time before it happened. Kate knew it was inevitable and she tried her best to be as cordial as possible. She may not have had the kind of money that Jared Taylor had access to growing up, but her parents made sure that she was raised with at least *some* sense of decorum and congeniality. "There are times when the only things princely that a pauper can afford are good manners and a bar of soap," her mother said. Clean and well-mannered. Kate modified that into "sculpted and calculating" over the years, but since arriving in Iowa, she seemed to be losing her edge.

When Jared Taylor announced that he was bringing his mother and that he wanted to stay at the farm while they were there, however, she couldn't help herself. "Oh, sure Jared, no problem...I'll just find somewhere else to stay while you are here. Maybe you can spring for a hotel room for me while you visit, oh that's right, there is no hotel! No, it won't be a problem, I have a friend I can stay with. Oh, how about Tuesday Wells? Is she coming too? Sure, the guest bedroom is prepared and ready to go!" She made it through three-quarters of the conversation before resorting to snide comments, so she counted that as progress. She would go through with it, she would live through it, and she would call Maeve.

Kate was nervous. She hadn't talked to Maeve since the week before Thanksgiving, hadn't been in the bakery and other than Em, hadn't seen any patients. In her frame of reference, that meant she was friendless. It had happened before, right before the move to Iowa. She thought of the group of women that she drank wine with, her friends.

Leaning over marble counter tops, discussing the horrors of getting caught wearing the same thing twice and who rubbed elbows and sometimes *more* than elbows, with the jet set royalty du jour. No one ever talked about anything, really. The conversations over dinner had so much fluff in them they made the soufflés that sat in front of them look dense as bricks. So when she announced that she was leaving Jared Taylor and the invitations for brunches and parties stopped coming in, Kate just conceded that the friendships were over and moved ahead.

But Maeve was different. Maeve was in your face. She was a bulldog friend. Opinionated and unpretentious. Big shouldered and bossy. That Irish woman could have had no earthly idea how much she meant to Kate. Until she picked up the phone to dial her, Kate had no earthly idea herself.

"Yes?" Maeve answered the phone quietly, and it took Kate a moment to realize it was her.

"Maeve?"

"Well who else would it be?" the voice on the other end replied.

Kate cleared her throat and began "I deserve it, Maeve. Whatever you have, throw it at me. I am horrible, snobby, self-centered and mean. I am so sorry. So sorry that I embarrassed you, so sorry that I made fun of you and Wall-errr-- Mr. Jawolski. So sorry."

"Oh, shut up already! Thank you!!" Maeve exclaimed.

"What?" Kate asked, surprised by Maeve's demeanor

"Thank you for setting me straight, Kate. You were right," Maeve replied.

"About what?"

"About everything. I have been using my father as an excuse to hide from the world, I have been waiting for "Mr. Right" to come to me and he was right there in front of me all this time. Well, I guess it's fitting that you are the first to know this...Wally and I have a date tomorrow night," the excitement in her voice was evident. "Oh, *and* because you puked all over my car, I had the incentive to finally clean that beast out!

"I said all that to you? Really?" Kate said, almost afraid to hear the answer.

"Yes, you don't remember? Oh, the V-Greats. Kate, I should be the one with the apology. Carla warned me to go easy on you. I'm sorry that I have not been the greatest influence on you."

“I am talking to Maeve Right? You are using Wally instead of Mr. Jawolski after all,” Kate laughed.

“Look, Kate, I said some things that were way out of line and...”

“Stop, just stop. It's fine. I'm all right, but I do need your help with something.”

“Anything, Kate. You name it.”

“Do you have a couch I could crash on?”

CHAPTER NINETEEN

The visit was short. Jared Taylor left right after Christmas and although even a brief visit was longer than Kate was comfortable with, especially since Jared Taylor, his mistress and his mother were all spending the holiday under her roof, she was proud of the way she handled it. Maeve and her father invited her to spend Christmas with them, and that helped. Opening presents was not a huge part of Christmas for the Swifton family anyhow. When you could afford to buy anything you wanted, whenever you wanted, Christmas kind of lost its magic.

She would give the children gifts, though, just not from St. Nick, since what she referred to as the "Santa Myth" was never instilled in them. She felt like she was lying if she told her children to behave because if they didn't, the jolly old elf would not bring them gifts. That was extortion as far as she was concerned. Even the Christmas carols bothered her. *You better watch out. You better not cry,*" Kate credited with being responsible for more than half of the childhood emotional issues known to modern psychology. She thought that she might have a talk with Carla about grabbing something when she and the girls from the beauty shop went to Chicago for the after Christmas deals. It wasn't really time sensitive, and she thought it would be nice to have some "start over in Iowa presents" anyhow.

If anyone could have been blamed for her change of heart, it would be Maeve. Spending time with Maeve and her father for the holiday made her realize how much she'd missed the simple traditions that she'd grown up with. Christmas didn't have to be lavish. She thought of the holidays spent with her family when she was younger, and it awakened a sense of what her kids could still experience. There were a lot of changes that she would have to make before she was ready to embrace the idea completely.

At some point during the holidays, Kate quit calling her soon-to-be-ex "Him." She was done fighting. Whatever the cause of the marriage failing, it was done. She knew that her motivations for staying as long as she did were entirely selfish. She liked the life she had enough to put up with what she had to; to continue to place blame would be pointless now. Whether it was the time spent at Maeve's house or the ache in her heart from missing her children, she didn't know, but she was starting to soften a little, and it scared her.

Her cell phone had taken a tumble into the bath at Maeve's and although she had a few hours to make the trip into the city for a new one, she decided to send for one instead. Jared Taylor would be leaving the farm to head for the flight back to California, and she could go back home. The kids would be waiting for her there, Carla had volunteered to come watch them and serve as a buffer between Jared Taylor leaving and Kate arriving, and no phone call was more important than getting back to hug her children.

There was no cell service at the house anyway, and she actually started to like the quiet. Being reachable at all times, and for any reason, was something she thought of as sort of a moral obligation. Forgoing her life "on call" meant she had to give up the idea that she was all that important. Carla assured her that anyone worth talking to would call her back, now she had an excuse to carve out time for herself, and she could decide who to give her house phone number to. It was foreign to her, but she was beginning to appreciate the beauty of not having to take time out to recharge as often, because she was just not plugged-in as much.

❧

The heat is fixed upstairs now.

Don't forget to keep the thermostat set at 68 and no higher as it dries out the mucous membranes and is not good for the children's skin if it is set above that--it will dry your skin out, as well; extra moisturizer wouldn't hurt.

Deli meat is not considered a suitable source of protein. Make sure you keep an eye on Stella, she looks like she's gained some weight.

Kate sighed, there were sticky notes left all over the house where she would be sure to see them. All reminders of what he thought she was doing wrong or not capable of doing herself. It raised her blood pressure a bit, but she was used to that form of communication. Jared Taylor hated to use the phone to text, yet he loved the idea of placing yellow reminders for her all over the place.

Mr. and Mrs. Langsbough will be attending dinner this evening. Do not wear blue, and do not mention anything about Patricia Mills, it would be embarrassing for them.

That was the first such note she had ever received. She was 27 years old and they had only dated a short while. Kate, not at all fond of receiving orders, approached Jared Taylor about it.

"Look, Kate, I am not trying to insult you, I am trying to *insulate* you. The people we surround ourselves with are ruthless and have a memory that will outlast anything you can imagine. One misstep, one slight, real or imagined and your life will be miserable. I do not want to make your life any harder, I am just trying to keep you from making enemies by accident."

"You have some kinda friends, Jared," Kate quipped, as she tried to memorize the note.

"Exactly," he replied.

The notes had become a part of her life. They did not have to *stay* a part of her life. She went through the house and wadded up yellow square after yellow square and threw them away.

Kate's personal favorite was the one she found stuck just inside her nightstand drawer she found as she was relocating the contents of the guest bedroom from downstairs: "*Kate, I miss you. We don't have to do this, do we?*" scribbled in Tuesday Wells' signature "Fuchsia" lipstick liner. She threw the pillow over her face as she fell backward onto the bed laughing. The thought of Jared Taylor and "Tuesday" possibly sharing the same bed was buffered by the tell-tale sloppiness of his handwriting. Kate knew it was scribbled quickly in what she assumed was an act of desperation, and she almost felt like "The Other Woman" of "The Other Woman" and for the brief moment between closing her eyes and nodding off to sleep, she felt like everything would work out for the best, after all.

CHAPTER TWENTY

Kate woke up on New Year's Day with her head aching and back stiff, although it was not from pre-birthday parties or V-Greats. Maeve had been busy with Wally lately, Kate suspected they were getting serious, but she did not pry. She needed the week after Christmas to re-group anyhow. After waking with a start to squeals of delight coming from downstairs, Kate's mood lightened when she remembered what day it was and she giggled as she realized her pajamas now consisted of a worn pair of boxer shorts and a t-shirt instead of the latest from Victoria's Secret. The thought of donning a pair of Ray Bans and sliding across the floor to the tune of a Bob Seger Song crossed her mind. Liberating.

The shrieks were coming from beside the 6 ft. cedar still standing in the back corner of the living room. In the Swifton household, the tree was always taken down by the help and put away Christmas evening after everyone went to sleep. By the time the family opened their eyes on December 26th, there was not a trace of Christmas left in the house. Kate wanted to keep all of the decorations up until the sixth of January like her mother always did, although she had forgotten the reason for the tradition, it seemed a nice enough length of time to have it in the house. She had the lights and trim on the tree before Jared Taylor and his mother arrived for their stay. She was always quite good about marking her territory and the Christmas decorations were no exception. They were guests in *her* house, she made sure to leave little room for doubt about that. It was the first time she had decorated a tree in years, and she was quite impressed with her efforts. The unpacking of the ornaments was something she always looked forward to, but had not done in years. She used ornaments she'd stored in the basement for over a decade rather than the new ones she normally would have someone else go out and buy or whatever pre-lit, plastic-needled display she managed to pick up.

"MOMMOMMOMOMOM!!!!"

Santa Claus and his elves made it to Iowa. Son-of-a-gun. She had left the kitchen door open a crack overnight, and the steps of tiny reindeer traced with what must have been an eyebrow pencil filled with glitter along with the tell-tale sign of footprints from the bottom of a pair of Keen's belonging to Carla went from the door to the living room. The faint smell of ammonia made Kate smile. Carla and the girls had really gone all out. It was Carla's idea to surprise the kids, not Kate's. When the children had their slumber party at Carla's the night of Kate's "bowling alley-eey" revelation, she was shocked when the children told her Santa had never been to their house; they got sweaters and Savings Bonds, but those were from their grandparents.

"Looks like Santa is based out of Chicago this year, mom! Look! The tags are still on the train set! Coool!" J.T. immediately set about putting the tracks down and configuring his train depot.

Kate smiled, she knew he didn't believe in Santa or the Tooth Fairy, but it didn't have to be the same with Stella, Carla convinced her of that. She appreciated the way J.T. played along. When Kate was preparing him for Christmas morning, she was expecting back talk. What she got was a laugh and "*Cool.* I get more presents this way, right?"

"Maybe he has an outlet store there or something, just in case the elves got overwhelmed, what do you think Stella?" she looked over to see her daughter wiping the tears from her eyes.

"Honey what's wrong? Are you not happy with your presents?" Kate knelt down to wipe the hair from her daughter's face.

"I knew I was right!" Stella cried.

"Right about what, sweetheart?" Kate tensed a little, looking around for something that might have given the secret away.

"I knew he was for real. I knew you and daddy told him you thought I had enough toys already and so he never came to our house. I knew that's why I only got sweaters!! Mom! This is great!! He came this time!!"

Kate hugged her daughter close and cried right along with her. Maybe a sense of wonder was really as important as anything else she could give her daughter. Kate smiled, maybe a sense of wonder would be a good thing for her, as well.

CHAPTER TWENTY-ONE

The birds were busy chirping in the trees just outside of Kate's window. Her initial inclination was to find an arborist to trim the limbs down a bit so they wouldn't be singing love songs directly outside her window. Rationally, Kate knew the chirping shouldn't bother her, that's what birds do, after all. However, Kate was not quite prepared to be greeted with such cheeriness. She was happier now, to be sure, but the trill-a-trilling of her fine feathered friends would take a while to appreciate. She rolled over and shielded her eyes from the sunlight streaming through. *Whose bright idea was it to leave the blackout curtains in the basement storage room anyhow?* When she realized it was her decision, she chalked it up to a momentary lapse of reason, and slowly rose from the bed and rolled her eyes.

The conversations she had been having with herself in the days following Jared Taylor's visit in December had somehow turned kinder and thankfully, quieter. The winter had been brutal; but like the old oak, whose roots had once arched above ground as if to gain the momentum to strike back down and grab the earth more deeply, it had released its grip during one long weekend of rain and warm temperatures. Kate walked to the other side of the room and looked out the window at it, scanning its length, noticing the roots were almost as long as the tree was tall. "So much hidden beneath the surface," she mused. *What am I going to do with that? What happens to dead trees? Do I have someone chop it up for firewood?* She didn't know, she came from a place where the palm trees lined the streets like little soldiers, guarding the concrete below them with absolute permanence and predictability.

As she was getting dressed, she could hear shrieks of laughter and yelling. No fighting? Was she still dreaming? She put on her shoes and coat, which in just two days had become a full season too warm for her, and headed out the door.

She froze in her tracks. Across the yard almost hugging each other were two children she vaguely recognized as her own. They were laughing and seemed unaware of her as she stood there motionless, completely taken by the sight of them. Curiosity eventually got the better of her and Kate went down the porch steps to investigate.

"Well now. How are we going to get it out?" Kate walked over and stood on the border of a large puddle with one purple boot stuck firmly in the middle of it. Stella was on the other side of the muddy pool, looking worried.

"I'm sorry mommy, I didn't mean to get it stuck, I promise, and J.T. was only trying to help."

"J.T., come over here and give me a hand will you?" Kate said as she looked down at the boot, trying to come up with a plan to get it out without turning the whole thing into a filthy, messy, ordeal.

"Mom, here, use this," said an almost unfamiliar voice behind her. She turned around to see J.T., holding a pitchfork out to her. He had grown 3 inches taller in just six short months, his voice had begun to deepen and he began to embrace the idea of being "the man of the house." Kate was so startled, she slipped on the muddy ground falling within arm's reach of the boot.

Stella ran around the puddle and hid behind J.T., only coming out from behind him when she heard the sound of giggling coming from the direction of the water. She peeked out from behind the blue rain slicker to see her mother covered with mud holding the boot victoriously up in the air. Stella started yelling at the top of her lungs, "My mom's the coolest, my mom's the coolest!" while jumping up and down with one dirty sock where the boot would have been.

Kate threw the boot in the direction of the house just as the horn from the white Ford Pickup truck sounded at the end of the driveway. She sat there contemplating her next move, which ultimately made no difference whatsoever, as dry land to anchor herself up with was nowhere near.

"Little early in the day for cooking class isn't it?" Sawyer said as he slowly got out of the truck, stepping carefully on the soft ground as he walked toward the mess.

"What?" Kate laughed, "You know it's never too early to teach the kids how to cook for themselves." Her eyes were invisible, partly from being covered in mud, and partly because she was grinning so big, they all but disappeared behind the apples of her cheeks.

"Wha?" J.T. and Stella said in unison, looking at the two adults in front of them, who obviously were in on some kind of joke.

"MUD PIES!" Kate laughed, as she scooped up a ball of mud and threw it back and forth between her hands. When she looked up, the shocked faces of her children caused her to pause. She thought perhaps her behavior was too much, and they might not be able to handle this much of a shift in her personality all at once. "Here. J.T., hang on to the end of the pitchfork and help hoist me out of this mess," she said, regaining her composure a bit.

She looked down for a place she could rest on one hand as her other hand waved about searching for the pitchfork handle. A gloved hand met hers instead and lifted her up and out effortlessly. Kate did not look up; she was not a romantic and had no intention of falling prey to the fairy tales she was told as a child. Sawyer was just being kind, but Kate knew emotional entanglements sometimes arose from innocence, and she was not about to add that problem to her list of things to deal with. Kate was not the helpless maiden being rescued by the knight on the white steed. In this case the maiden's divorce was still pending, the knight was still married to the love of his life, and as for the white steed, it was still limping around with a dent in its passenger side door. Kate kept her head low and started sweeping her hands across her clothes as if to wipe the dust off of them.

"Ma'am?"

"What?"

"That doesn't work so well with mud, it kind of rubs it in worse."

Kate stopped. Visions of the washcloth baths and rubbing the cruddy in further came back to her and she laughed, "Didn't anyone tell you my last name is Klutzinsky?"

"Oh! I might have guessed!" Sawyer laughed. "So you are related to the Trip-ah-lots aren't you?"

"Second Cousin, twice removed," Kate giggled as she steadied herself on his arm as she made her way to dry land.

"Here, you go clean up, I'll go back to town for a load of gravel to put on top of the mess and drop the kids off at school for you," Sawyer offered. "Then I'll get William out here to take care of that tree. My word, it's a good thing it fell the way it did, or we'd be bringing in a construction crew too."

Before she could protest, the kids were running full speed, oblivious to the moat of wet earth between them and their first ever ride in a truck. By the time she looked up, all three occupants were waving goodbye as the pickup pulled slowly out of the drive.

CHAPTER TWENTY-TWO

The phone had been ringing from the time it took Kate to get out of her bathrobe, put a towel over her still wet hair, and slip into her sweats, which either meant it was either an overly determined telemarketer or Maeve. Deciding it must be Maeve, Kate picked it up.

"For goodness sake, woman, how long does it take you to get to a phone? Your house isn't that darn big, I nearly finished this whole Bear Claw waiting for you!"

"I just got out of the shower, Maeve, wait... Bear Claw?" Kate asked, expecting to hear the word cigarette.

"You know, I have lived in this town all this time and I never knew what a Bear Claw was. With all the fuss all the time about the kolaches, I just ignored the Bear Claw. But I think I like the Bear Claw just about as much!"

"Why Maeve, if I didn't know better, I would say you are warming up quite nicely to the baker of fine pastries!" Kate laughed as she was trying to towel dry her hair, transferring the phone receiver from one ear to the next as she did so being careful not to get the cord tangled up in the towel.

"Warming up? Maeve laughed. "Honey, I've been *preheated* for about 30 years now!!!"

"So when's the wedding?" Kate laughed as she fiddled with her own ring finger, trying to rub away the faint tan line still visible from her recent weekend trip to California. She went to have a heart to heart with her divorce lawyer, and she came back with a broken one. Nothing had changed, Jared wasn't budging. It was not until she got back from California and had time to think long and hard about whether she was willing to stay married in name only, and put up with infidelity, or remove the wedding band once and for all.

There was silence. Kate had been so caught up in her own thoughts, she had forgotten she was talking to her friend and wondered if she had accidentally hung up on Maeve. After realizing the phone had to actually be put back on it's cradle to hang up, she smiled for a second and said, "Never thought I would be grateful for this old piece of junk."

"He is *not* a piece of..." Bellowed the voice on the other line, causing Kate to trip on the towel as it made its way to the floor. "I can't believe you aren't happy for me; I can't believe I was going to ask you to be my maid of honor! You think *all* men are jerks! Well, let me tell you, missy, just because *you* married one, doesn't mean all of 'em are! I am so..."

"You're getting *married*? Wait! Wait! Wait! I was talking about this old phone, not Wally!"

"Oh, *I know*, that old thing! I do love the color, though. Pops had his taken out of the wall in '92, you would have thought he was sending his only son off to war, he was so sad about it, but the contractor wouldn't work around it when they remodeled the kitchen so. Yeah, So, it's a good thing I have four brothers!" Maeve laughed.

Kate sat down at the kitchen table and took a deep breath. She had to remember she was talking to *Maeve*, which meant the conversation could well go on for another hour before the topic of her impending nuptials would come back around.

"Maeve, Maeve, MAEVE!"

"Yup? What?"

"Wally!"

"Oh! We are getting married at St. Ludmila during the festival, everyone we know will be there anyway."

"Oh, Maeve! How perfect! I am so happy for you both! How did he propose?"

"Propose? He was supposed to do that wasn't he?" Maeve laughed. "Well, he started to I guess...he was talking about how bread needed yeast to rise, how cake needed baking powder to rise, and by that time I thought he was talking all sexy, so I told him "Hold on a minute there, mister. No more talk of cooking something up until I'm married!" Maeve let out an enormous laugh as she said,

"Imagine my surprise when he pulls a ring out of the flour bin and asks me if I will be his baking soda!"

Kate was laughing so hard she decided the floor would be the safest place to be. She was listening to every detail, kicking her legs up and down like a 6th grader talking about boys, twisting the phone cord around her fingers, waiting to hear more. "Oh, the Baker's church! Good for Wally! I'm just glad he didn't ask you to be his *sourdough starter*!"

They were both crying from laughing so hard and after the sighs became longer and softer, then finally ended, there was a long silence.

"Maeve?"

"Yah huh?"

"I am so completely and utterly happy for you both, congratula—Oh! Man! He's back! How long have we been talking? Maeve, I have to let you go, I'll stop by the office later! Sawyer just pulled up and I'm not even done getting ready.....uh, for my day. Getting ready for my day, yes!" Kate knew Maeve was too caught up in her own moment to notice the slip, and Kate was relieved she didn't have to explain something she couldn't even explain to herself.

CHAPTER TWENTY-THREE

The white pickup pulled into the driveway and Sawyer got out of the cab slowly. "Someone looks like the cat that got the canary," he said as he lifted the tools from the back of his truck. The brim of his hat sat low over his brow and Kate could not see his eyes. She could not tell by the sound of his voice alone whether the remark was in jest or curiosity.

She watched him throw out garden hoses and tools, and other items she had no name for, let alone knowledge of its use. He was quiet. Not the quick-witted cowboy she was getting to know, but silent, concentrating on his task as if he were trying to avoid conversation. She sensed something was wrong, but found herself in the uncomfortable position between knowing someone and knowing someone well enough to ask if there was something going on, so she waited.

Sawyer finally looked up to throw some metal pipe around the front of the truck when she caught a glimpse of his eyes. They were red and swollen, and she felt a pang of panic rise up from her gut. How was she supposed to react? Should she come up and give him a hug? Should she ask him what was wrong? There was no playbook on this, there were no rules of etiquette, or if there was, Lillian Eichler had failed to address them in her book.

To her relief, she did not have to do anything, because the next words out of her mouth had nothing to do with Sawyer, nothing to do with her, but had to do with the massive piece of equipment being rolled down a ramp and onto her front of her muddied lawn.

“What in the world is that?”

“You've telling me you don't know what this is?” Sawyer said.

“It looks like a lawnmower on steroids mated with the shark from Jaws.”

“It’s a rototiller, for the *garden*, to turn over the earth...for the love of Pete, are you telling me you have never planted anything outside?”

Kate blushed. Just what was she going to say? The truth? That the closest she got to digging a garden was when the underside of her fingernails got dirty from cleaning the organic vegetables she got from Trader Joe's? Seriously. There was no way for her to save face, so she didn't say anything.

“I'm sorry, I shouldn't have made fun of you,” Sawyer started.

"Don't worry about it, have you heard the news?" Kate asked, still eyeing the gasoline powered garden hoe with suspicion.

"Yes, I just found when I went into town," Sawyer said as he walked around the front of the tiller. "How did you find out so soon, it just happened this morning?"

"Maeve called me, you must have spoken to Wally already. Isn't it great?"

"What?" Sawyer looked shocked as he turned to her, "You know; I knew you didn't like it here. I even suspected you and Em didn't get along, but really? Kate?" Sawyer closed the truck's tailgate and turned to leave.

"Sawyer wait! What do you mean we don't get along? Who says I don't like it here?"

Kate ran in front of the driver's side door, stopping Sawyer from putting his hand on the door handle. She shocked herself, not sure where the sudden intensity had come from, and she had no idea what to do or say next. Sawyer looked startled, but not angry. He braced himself, his arms were straight against the truck but he was close enough that she could tell the color of his eyes. Green. They were green as the hills of Ireland. *Ireland...Maeve!*

"Maeve and Wally!" Kate blurted, you aren't happy for them, Sawyer?"

"Maeve and Wally, what are you talking about? I was talking about Em."

The red eyes, the silence, it was about Em? Her eyes darted back and forth like a typewriter carriage processing what had just happened. Then she looked up, straight at Sawyer and shook her head. Sawyer looked down at the ground and nodded and with one hand on her shoulder he drew her in and they hugged each other, crying freely. Kate had not been held in an embrace like that for so many years, she did not want to let go. The relief of having a shoulder to lay her head on was so comforting, she almost forgot about Em. That moment, just knowing there was another human with the strength to just hold her, shook her to the core. Suddenly she felt guilty, what was she doing? Em was really just a patient to her, but Sawyer had just lost a friend. He was the one who needed solace and Kate did not know how to deal with how *she* felt. She did not feel guilty enough, however, to want to stop the embrace.

Blessed are those who mourn, for they shall be comforted.

Kate stiffened at the sound of her grandmother's voice, it had been months since she had heard it. *Easy for you to say, you're already dead, Gran.* She looked at Sawyer, hoping she had not said it out loud.

He let her go, and with one hand still on her shoulder, he took the other and grabbed the door handle on the truck, and said, "I won't be coming back into work today, Kate, I have a funeral to plan."

“Of course,” Kate stepped back, wiping the tears from her eyes, “I am so sorry, Sawyer, I had no idea you two were so close.”

“Em's husband died about the same time as my wife had her...” Sawyer stopped and looked down, his shoulders started to shake and he started to cry again. Kate wanted to say something, wanted him to stop crying, but she stood motionless, wary of moving or saying anything that might make things worse.

After what seemed like forever, Sawyer took a deep breath and said, “Yes, we were close. I'll see you the day after tomorrow, then.”

Kate stood in the driveway and watched him leave, feeling as if her heart was as uprooted as the tree beside her. She stood there, alone and crying until the sound of thunder in the distance warned her. She had been cautioned not to stand outside during thunderstorms, but she stayed there until the raindrops touched her face and commingled with her tears before going back inside.

CHAPTER TWENTY-FOUR

Em's funeral was simple but heartfelt. The people of the community set up potluck dishes and paper plates in the hall and mingled. It seemed to Kate to be about as joyous as her wedding reception and she felt oddly familiar with the atmosphere she was surrounded by as she watched old ladies touch each other's elbows in half hugs of shared grief and sympathy. Maeve pointed out to Kate that only one of Em's daughters made it to the funeral. She looked overwhelmed by the amount of people who were there.

"Looks like she didn't actually anticipate quite so many folks to pay their respects," Kate whispered to Maeve.

"She favors her mother, doesn't she?" Maeve said, as she sat down with a plate full of potatoes salad and orange Jell-O with carrot shavings floating inside.

"I suppose so, I didn't know what her father looked like," Kate murmured.

"Sawyer inherited the house, Em's daughter has her own life out west, so she is letting him have it, generous, eh?" Maeve said as she popped a piece of apple turnover into her mouth.

"I don't know…I guess?" Kate replied.

"You know, Em was happier than she had been in years lately, she was even...nice. I heard she decided to take up painting again, maybe that was it," Maeve poked the molded gelatin trying unsuccessfully to stab a carrot strand Kate smiled. It had made a difference. *She* made a difference. For the first time in a long time, she felt like she mattered.

"Maeve?" Kate said, unconsciously chastising her friend for such poor table manners.

"What? What?" I don't like carrots!" Maeve said, not looking up.

Kate smiled. She had never known anyone before who was able to tell what she was thinking just by the tone of her voice. *That* was an art crafted only from those who got close enough to someone to see underneath the surface where the cobwebs and chewed pieces of gum were stuck. *That* only came from those who cared enough to actually look.

"It's been a while since we've had a funeral here, in town," Maeve said, trying hard to chew with her mouth closed. The urge to talk forced her to use her hand to hide her mouth so she could do both. "They usually get taken to the funeral home out of town and most of us aren't able to take a day off of work, so we don't really ever get to say goodbye."

Kate thought about it for a moment. She had never been to a funeral before. She was just a toddler when her grandfather had passed, and since she could not bear to go to her grandmother's funeral, she pretended she was too ill to go. She knew it was a horrible thing to do, but she also knew her grandmother would not be upset. She would have understood perfectly.

“I didn't say goodbye,” Kate heard herself say. She looked up at Maeve hoping she hadn't noticed.

“We need someone to help put the folding chairs away, I need to see about taking a plate home to dad, *of course, you are saying goodbye, you're here, aren't ya? Besides, it ain't like it's forever or anything,*” Maeve made the sign of the cross and started in on her potato salad. Of course, she noticed. She was Maeve.

Kate smiled through the tears as they made their way down the sides of her nose; she could say goodbye. Em, Jared Taylor, even her grandmother. Without even realizing it, Kate's friend had said exactly the right thing. It was time to let go.

CHAPTER TWENTY-FIVE

There were no sticky notes to remind her that she needed to go through her filing cabinet. No yellow square to encourage her to get it over with. "Okay, well then, let's have a look," Kate said aloud as she lifted the manila envelopes out of the file drawer.

The divorce papers. She also hadn't gotten around to seeing if there was a lawyer in the area willing to take this on. She could not afford any more round trips to California just to have someone look over documents. For every one thousand she negotiated for in the final settlement draft, it seemed to cost her hundreds of dollars just to submit the paperwork, so if she found someone within driving distance, at least, she would save on airfare. A smile crossed her face as she went over to the alcove by the phone, reaching over stacks of bills and school work, she picked up the phone book and mused,

"Who knows? I might even read the front of it."

The smile had not waned as she started to organize the stacks of documentation until she started reading through the first few paragraphs of the final draft of the divorce complaint. She had read it before but paid little attention. It stated she was now responsible for the property taxes on the land and she was also liable for any expenses incurred in the move. She was speechless. She could not even cry out in anger, her throat was suddenly as dry as the paper she held in her hands. He had her. She knew it was legal, she knew he had a right, and yet, she was still surprised by it.

She had no way to pay the taxes. She hadn't seen an assessment on the property, but her one and only client was gone and no other patients were lined up, so she had no income regardless of how low the taxes might be. Every penny was strictly accounted for until the divorce was final. However, there was a stipulation. If she agreed to move back to California so Jared Taylor could be closer to the children, the taxes would be paid, she would retain ownership of the farm and her travel expenses would be provided for, so she could visit there anytime she liked. The answer seemed clear.

Going back to California seemed the only logical course. Kate had come to love Iowa, but who was she kidding? *Jared Taylor was right.* No one cared about her opinion, professional or otherwise. The emptiness in her gut felt like a big, dark, pit of nothing. It was true. She was a fraud. If anyone found out who she *really* was, they would never try to get close to her. She was the unfeeling, aloof, imperious woman Jared Taylor always said she was.

She would tell Maeve first, then Wally and Carla, of course. Kate's stomach flipped. Sawyer. Her heart ached a little. Here was a man who was so in love with his wife, that he stayed faithful in spite of everything, *for years.*

Jared Taylor couldn't make it *four days*. Telling her friends she was leaving would be hard, but admitting to Sawyer she was giving up, seemed impossible.

Do not make decisions out of fear. If you do, fear will be your master, and fear never sleeps, and it never gives up. "Okay, Gran, as far as I know, that one's not in the Bible, so I'll give you the credit. I'm a coward, though, I've never really felt brave. I'm not like you were."

There's a first time for everything, kiddo.

There had to be another answer, there had to be another way. If not now, then soon, so what she really needed was time. Kate looked up and shook her head, "Okay, I'm going to give this another try, but I'm telling You, if this is what having faith feels like, I can't say that I like it one bit."

CHAPTER TWENTY-SIX

Maeve looked at Kate's hands and shook her head. "For the love of all that's holy! Will you just *stop it*, already?"

"What?" Kate replied, ignoring Maeve's instructions to stop picking the paint off of the front porch steps. She concentrated on getting the edges first, then peeled off a strip or two. She stopped after a sharp piece of aged latex found its way under her fingernail, causing her to curse and look up at Maeve in dismay.

"Just how in the blue blazes do you think you are going to make it by working at the Mighty Mart? They only pay minimum wage, you know." Maeve blew a stray strand of hair from her face as she situated herself on the bottom step in front of Kate.

"I know, but it would be something, besides, it would only be until you get back from the honeymoon...really, I mean if you aren't around, I'll have nothing to do anyhow."

"You are a psychologist, Kate, and you'd be too busy analyzing a person's choice of take-out instead of ringing them up at the register." Maeve took the wisp of hair that kept finding her nose and twirled it around her finger before finding a place for it behind her ear. "Besides, you haven't exactly been looking for clients now, have you? I personally think Wally and I could use some premarital counseling because I am not so sure he knows exactly what he's signing up for. I'm not exactly high maintenance, but still."

Kate shook her head and took a sip out of the water bottle she started carrying with her whenever she knew she was going to be around Maeve. Her eyes followed her feet as she pointed her toes together, then out, before she turned her attention back to Maeve.

"C'mon, you guys were made for each other, between your Irish sensibilities and Wally's flour soul salvation, I'd say it's a match made in heaven. If there *is* such a thing."

Maeve bent over and grabbed a handful of grass, threw it at Kate and laughed. "Okay, well you have me there...but I know plenty of people here in town who could really use your help, I mean it Kate. Don't settle for the Mighty Mart when you could be doing some real good here."

"What exactly am I supposed to do? Advertise?"

"Have you forgotten how small this town is, Kate? All I need to do is go get my hair done and you will have clients in no time flat. The best way to get the word out around here is to talk to your hairdresser," Maeve put on hand on her hip and ran the other through her massive mane of fiery curls, then continued, “I'll talk to Carla about setting up an appointment when I get back to town.”

“You really think that will work, don't you?” Kate shook her head at the idea. “I'll hand it to you, Maeve, you do think outside the box.”

“That's what you get when you are raised within a stone's throw of a dozen silos, honey. There aren't many boxes to think *in,*” Maeve grinned. “Remember who you are, Kate, and if you can't remember, then find out. Don't let yourself down just because someone else has. You are not who Jared Taylor thinks you are, you are not who your parents believe you are. Honestly, you’re not even who *I* think you are, although I bet I'm closer to being right than the rest of 'em combined.” Maeve got up and motioned with her hands for Kate to get up and give her a hug goodbye.

Kate was still standing with her arms out a little, embracing the space her friend had just held when she thought about asking what a silo was, but by the time she opened her mouth, Maeve was gone. Lowering her arms back to her sides, Kate looked over the front yard and to the outbuildings forming a semi-circle on the other end of the driveway. She imagined a barn full of hay and maybe a farm cat or two, she might even learn how to milk a cow. Whistling “Old Mac Donald Had a Farm,” she turned around and went back up the steps of the house just as the phone started to ring.

CHAPTER TWENTY-SEVEN

The couple sank into the couch in Kate's office, trying unsuccessfully to stretch their feet to the ground; missing the floor just enough that they kept pointing their toes downward, searching for solidity. They leaned on each other like puzzle pieces that look similar but don't quite fit, exchanging glances of disapproval as they volleyed for the most comfortable position.

Kate smiled at them and sat down on the chair in front of them. "Can I get you some coffee or tea?" she asked, setting out two cups on her desk.

"No, no thank you," the couple said in unison.

"Well, then," Kate started, "you told me a little bit on the phone last night, Mr. and Mrs. Yoder, but I do have a few questions before we get going on this. You said that you have been together for 40 years, is that correct?"

"Yes," the woman said, pressing her hand into the man's arm, propping herself up straight.

"Okay then," Kate continued. "I also see here that you have been married for twenty years. So am I correct in saying, you two dated for twenty years before getting married?"

There was silence for a few moments, then the man leaned forward and started to say something, then stopped and looked up and shook his head. The woman looked down at the floor and mumbled under her breath, then looked at Kate, "We didn't exactly ever date, Miss Brannigan."

"I see. Okay. I must have written something down wrong here," Kate looked over her notes.

"No, no," Mrs. Yoder said. "You wrote everything down correctly, it's just that it's very hard to explain."

"What is?" Kate asked.

"Well, *we* are," Mr. Yoder said. "We were together, but we never really dated." Mrs. Yoder poked her elbow into his ribs and he cleared his throat. "That is we were together, but not in the way you kids mean it. We were never alone together, not until our honeymoon." His eyes twinkled a little and he smiled and looked at his wife. "She was 16 when we met. My sister had some friends over the same night I came back from college on spring break. It was my freshman year."

"Daddy did not like him *at all,*" the woman laughed and slapped her thin leg. "I never knew why he couldn't stand him, but I wasn't interested at the time anyway, I was sure I was going to marry Elvis."

Kate grinned and said, “Well, let's get started, then. What brings you here to see me today?”

Mr. Yoder held up his hand as if he were in grade school and said, “Oh, I'd like to start.”

“Go ahead, Mr. Yoder, what would you like to say?”

“I think we're here to find out what is wrong with us. We simply don't fight like everyone else seems to, and we are wondering if it's...normal?” He looked nervously at his wife as if he was checking to see if he'd put it correctly.

“Well, all couples disagree at times Mr. Yoder, it's all in how you handle those disagreements. I think I can assume you love each other and you don't have brawls on a regular basis, am I right?” Kate smiled.

Mrs. Yoder looked visibly relieved and took her husband’s hand in hers, patting the top of it. “See dear, I told you so! You watch too much of that reality TV, we are okay, those folks on those shows are the ones who are messed up.”

Kate tried not to laugh out loud, sensing the statement was said in all seriousness. She noticed the man was fussing with the collar on his neatly pressed shirt, grimacing as he did so. “Are you okay, Mr. Yoder?”

“Yes, yes, I'm all right, it's just that...” he started.

"It's just that I thought since we were going out for the day, that I wanted it to be perfect. I am afraid I used Niagara on him without telling him. He hates it when I do that," Mrs. Yoder offered.

Kate's mind raced, she searched for the right words to tactfully suggest an alternative plan. "Well, I think intimacy is a beautiful thing at any age, however when it comes to giving someone medicine without their permission…"

"I didn't feed my husband spray starch, sweetie," Mrs. Yoder interrupted. "That would just be silly."

Mr. Yoder chimed in, "Intimacy! Ha! With my collar as stiff as it is, I can't even lean in to kiss her!"

The couple laughed, seemingly oblivious that Kate had misunderstood them entirely, forgetting there was such a thing as spray starch and Viagra now seemed to be named so very appropriately.

"Well, I'm glad we have that cleared up, I would say you two are the perfect example of a well-suited couple...pretty rare to see these days."

Mr. Yoder laughed, "When you know someone as well as we know each other, there is not a lot to argue about. I know I'm not going to change her, and she can't change me either, so since we know what we'd say to each other anyhow, we don't waste time fighting about anything.

Besides, we had twenty years to decide whether we were right for each other, and it turns out, we are."

"Twenty years, yes, about that...why did you decide to marry after twenty years of being together?" Kate asked.

"We were together *here* for twenty years before we married," Mrs. Yoder pointed to her heart.

Kate looked up from her notebook and raised an eyebrow, "I don't understand."

"And there's another reason why we are here," Mr. Yoder said, ignoring Kate's inquiry. "We are concerned about our daughter, she's in an awful situation, and she's made us promise not to tell anyone, but she needs help, Dr. Brannigan, we don't know what to do."

"Oh. Oh. Okay, well..." Kate was taken aback and tried to retrace the conversation they had been having to see if she could glean any helpful information before opening her mouth. There was nothing she could think of that would make her sound any more knowledgeable, so she just leaned in and asked, "How can I help?"

"We would like to see if we can make another appointment to see you, and ask if she could come along too. We'll see if she will drive us here, which will, at least, get her here safely," Mrs. Yoder's eyes were starting to well up and her chin was quivering slightly.

“Well, I can't see how it would hurt, is there anything more you can tell me about the situation that may be helpful?” Kate asked.

“No, we can't say anything, we promised,” Mr. Yoder said quietly. “Can we make our appointment for the same time next week, will that be okay?”

“Certainly, no problem, I'll write you in now,” Kate said, getting out her appointment book.

Mr. Yoder worked his way slowly to the edge of the couch, then pumped his legs as if he were on a swing and managed to get his feet to the floor. He stood up and turned, then took his wife's hand gently and helped her up and off the couch to hers.

They said their goodbyes and left. Kate, bouncing her pen up and down against the top of the desk, was left as confused as she was curious.

CHAPTER TWENTY-EIGHT

Kate stopped in to see Wally, with fresh resolve to limit herself to two trips a week for pastries, but unlimited access to her friend's advice and corny jokes.

"Wally, I don't even know these people, they just called out of the blue and made an appointment. You don't think Maeve is behind this do you?" Kate asked, not realizing she had started the conversation in her head until the baker gave her a quizzical look.

"Maeve?"

"Never mind, I'll go ask her myself, but tell me, what do you think of a couple who have been together for forty years and only married for twenty?" Kate said as she took a moistened finger to the sugar glaze on her pastry and put it in her mouth.

"What do I think?" Wally asked, amused. "Well I think they must be two of the smartest people I've heard of in a long time, that's what I think!"

"Hmm." Kate shook her head and blew Wally a kiss as she walked out the door. "Bye now, Mr. Jawolski, I'm going to take my "nice buns" out of here and go see that beautiful fiancé of yours."

"Hubba, hubba!" Wally called out, laughing.

Making her way to Maeve's office, stopping at the beauty shop window only long enough to wave hello, she turned the corner and knocked on Maeve's door."

"I'm in, now you come in!" Maeve shouted.

"Hey there, Maeve, how's the bride-to-be?" Kate said, smiling.

"How am I?" Maeve looked astonished. "How am I? Are you feeling okay Kate?"

"I'm okay, what did I do now?" Kate asked, bracing herself for one of Maeve's lectures.

"Nothing. Do you realize that in the whole time I have known you, you have not once come into this office without a complaint, this is the first time you have ever asked me how I am doing? So, I'll ask again, Kate, are you sure you are okay?" Maeve got up from her chair and gave Kate a hug.

"Wow. I never realized I was quite *that* self-absorbed."

"Well, of course, you wouldn't know, Kate. Besides, who's keeping track?" Maeve turned to sit back down.

Kate shook her head and sat down in the chair in front of the desk. "Obviously, *you* are, silly. I have to hand it to you, Maeve, you work fast! I no sooner stepped back into the house after you left yesterday when I got a phone call for an appointment!"

"Really?"

"So tell me, did you recommend couples counseling to Carla too? I don't mind, I just was not expecting it. They were so nice, Maeve, and they have a daughter and they booked for another appointment next week, thank you very much!"

"Your welcome, but I didn't do anything."

"Oh come on now, just accept the fact that you are an excellent friend and an amazing person who really knows how to come up with the most interesting ways to get things done."

"Well, yes…I am all that, but seriously, I didn't do anything."

"What do you mean? I know I heard you say you were going to talk to Carla when you went in for an appointment."

"You said you got the phone call right after I left. Now I admit to being somewhat of a lead foot, but even I could not have pulled that off, besides, does this hair *look* like it's been done yet?" Maeve looked up at the fiery fringe entwining itself with her eyelashes, moving up and down a little every time she blinked.

"I don't understand. How could that be? We were just talking about..." Kate felt the heat rising to her face, she was glad she was sitting down.

"Who were they? Or do you have to practice that whole doctor-patient confidentiality thing with me?"

"Actually, yes. Yes, I do have to practice that whole doctor-patient confidentiality thing with you."

"Okay, I'll just wait and find out when I actually do get this mop taken care of."

"If I didn't know better, I'd say Carla was an agent for the CIA, she knows news almost before it happens. What did they teach her in cosmetology school *...Perms and Intelligence Gathering 101: Covert Operations While Back Combing*?"

"Only my hairdresser knows for sure, love."

Kate got up and turned to Maeve, "Thank you."

"Again, your welcome, and again, for what?" Maeve laughed.

"For believing in me. For telling me the truth and being a friend," Kate smiled.

“Shucks.”

“Now *that's* a word I haven't heard in a while.”

“No. I mean it. We have to teach you how to shuck this summer, you are not an Iowan until you've learned to pull the outer leaves from an ear of corn.”

“Not today I hope, or I'll be the one needing the therapist.”

“Go now, before I start planning on how I'm going to get you bucking hay,” Maeve laughed.

Kate smiled. “Iowan.” *Who would have ever thought it?*

CHAPTER TWENTY-NINE

Seven days seemed more like seven years to her, but when the time came for the Yoders to return to Kate's office, she still felt unprepared. She had spent the week running different scenarios over and over in her head, rehearsing her responses and suggestions in front of the mirror, taking off her reading glasses and dangling them from one hand as she held her elbow in the other. She felt like an attorney ready to present closing arguments in a case with unknown charges, to a jury of her ghosts. She pictured her father sitting there with his nose in a newspaper, her mother playing with her St. Christopher medal, Jared Taylor's mom rolling her eyes and looking at her watch, and Jared Taylor sitting there with three plane tickets and divorce papers waiting for her to sign. She did not want the Yoders to suspect they were only the second client she'd ever had, although they were. Kate took great care to appear to be confident, even though she wasn't. It was all starting to feel like a lie, which was something she wasn't prepared for.

Being uncomfortable with being self-fabricated was new to her. Inventing yourself, writing your own back story, and learning to live a life that fulfilled the expectations of others for fear of losing the status quo, was a trait she had acquired over the years. It was not easy living a life others envied. It made Kate overly self-conscious about every move she made, from hair color to where she got her nails done. If it were a joke, it would have been a cruel one, but it was reality and somehow, okay. Because Kate really believed there was nothing she could have done to change it.

When the knock on her office door finally came, it still managed to startle her. She sat down in her chair quickly, crossed her legs, and grabbed her notebook.

“Come in!” she called out.

Mr. Yoder came in with a woman on his arm who looked nothing like what Kate had imagined. She was tall and thin, with waist length hair dyed so dark it looked blue against the florescent lighting. The woman kissed his cheek and turned to leave.

“Sylvie, stay, please? The doctor needs your input,” Mr. Yoder looked up at Kate.

“My name is Dr. Brannigan,” Kate stood up and put out her hand.

“Sylvie,” the young woman said, letting her hand fall limply into Kate's.

“Well now, why don't we all have a seat and we'll get started, okay?” Kate motioned to the couch and realizing there was no other place to sit, offered the Yoder's daughter her own chair.

“Where are you going to sit?” Sylvie said, her eyes cast downward.

“Oh, it's nothing, I'll just run across the hall and grab an extra, and I’ll be back in just a second.”

“Please, Dr. Brannigan, take my place,” Mrs. Yoder pleaded. “I have to run back down to the car, I forgot my reading glasses.”

“What do you need glasses for mom? I can go get them,” Sylvie looked up suspiciously.

“No honey, I need to walk anyway. The car ride was long, and my legs aren't ready for sitting just yet. Here. You sit by dad and Dr. Brannigan can have her chair back.”

“Look, folks, I have it already...now let's stop the musical chairs and get comfortable.” Kate had taken the opportunity to grab the wooden bench from the hallway and sat it beside her desk.

“Oh, mercy! I should have helped you with that!” Mr. Yoder cried.

“Nonsense. You should see me truck things around the farm when I'm in a mood. I'm practically the Hulk. You know, as in, *you wouldn't like me when I'm angry*,” Kate joked.

The room was silent. Kate looked around. All eyes were downcast and Mr. Yoder tried to sit up straight.

"Yes. Well," Kate said, taking a moment to recover from the failed attempt at lightening the mood, "The last time you were here, Mr. Yoder, you were telling me a little about how you and your wife met. We also talked a little about how couples handle disagreements in a variety of ways."

Sylvie shot up from her chair and looked straight at her parents. "What the hell is this about mom and dad? Is this some kind of set up? You two have never had a fight in your life! I wondered why we had to come all the way here just to see a doctor, do you even know what this means? Do you even know how much *trouble* I'm going to be in!?" Before anyone could say anything, she left the office, slamming the door behind her, leaving everyone in the room staring at each other uncomfortably.

"Well. Obviously, we have some more things to discuss now, don't we, Mr. and Mrs. Yoder?" Although she was visibly shaking, Kate tried to remain calm and direct. "It may very well have nothing to do with why you are here, but I am going to ask you anyhow, is your daughter alright? She seems very agitated and a bit distraught."

Mr. Yoder ignored the pleading look his wife was giving him and stood up. "I'm going to go look for Sylvie. She doesn't have the car keys, so she won't get very far."

Kate nodded her head, wondering where all of this was leading. "Mrs. Yoder, please, I need to know what is going on, in order to help."

"It's our daughter, she's gotten herself into a big mess, and we didn't know what else to do, so that's why we came here. It's her husband, Doctor Brannigan. He's a mean man. He keeps track of every move she makes, writes down the mileage every time she goes to the store, it's horrible and that's not the half of it."

"I see. I am so very sorry, Mrs. Yoder, but please, help me understand exactly why you thought I could be of help?" Kate leaned forward in her chair, resting her elbows on her knees and grabbed a tissue for Mrs. Yoder, who had broken into tears by the time Kate finished her question.

"Oh, it's not that we think you could *help*," Mrs. Yoder said, patting at the moisture as it cascaded down her cheek. "It's that you are far enough *away*. Sylvie's husband doesn't like that she has to drive us everywhere, but he also doesn't want to hire anyone else to do it, the cheapskate, so she drives us to our appointments, and so we arranged to have an appointment exactly two hours away. We told him you were the only one who would take our insurance, God forbid we should pay out of pocket and decrease the inheritance money. That's what he's waiting for. So he agreed."

"I still don't understand; didn't you drive yourselves the last time?"

"Yes, we told her husband it's cataracts, but we actually just saved the sunglasses from the last time we had our eyes dilated and he believed us. He's mean, but fortunately, he's not bright, so it worked. We drove ourselves the first time just to make sure we could see you regularly, with Sylvie. Since we're here, though, maybe you could help us come up with a plan?"

"A plan to what? A plan to...leave him?" Kate's heart started to beat in unison with the throb that had taken over the front of her head.

"Yes, six hours. That's what we need. Six hours can get her to the airport and on her way out east before he'll even know she's gone. All you have to do is convince Sylvie it's safe and the right thing to do. That is where you'll earn your paycheck, Dr. Brannigan. It will take some doing, but it will also ease that harebrained oaf of hers into the idea of this being a routine appointment, he won't suspect a thing when the time comes." Mrs. Yoder's eyes were dry now, and she looked steelier to Kate than she did when they first met.

"So, I'm sort of serving as a scapegoat? You don't really need my services?"

"We'd still have sessions, only you'll be seeing Sylvie too. Trust me, we still need counseling to help her through this, we still need you."

"What if I don't agree? What if I tell you I think this is highly suspect and unprofessional? What if I say I won't be a part of this? What then?"

"Oh, you won't disagree," Mrs. Yoder stated matter-of-factly.

"What makes you so sure?"

"Because I have a feeling you know exactly what it feels like to be her, that's why."

Kate tried to exhale, but the warm air stuck to her lungs, refusing to budge. She thought a sip of water would help dislodge it but she only wound up coughing, sending a spittle of Perrier into the air. She pounded on her chest, sat up straight and smoothed the imaginary wrinkles on her skirt.

"I apologize, must have gone down the wrong tube. Would you care for something to drink, Mrs. Yoder?"

Staring at the drops of water on the coffee table, Mrs. Yoder used the last of her tear-stained tissue to mop them up.

"No thank you. I had better get going. Dr. Brannigan, I am sorry to put you in this position. To be honest with you, a month ago, we would not have even considered coming here and doing this. Strange as it may sound to you, finding out you were here, just as we were losing all hope of ever helping our daughter, well I guess you could say you are an answer to a prayer."

Kate didn't mean to, but she let out a belly laugh, "*Me?* An answer to a prayer? You can't be serious." She stopped and looked at Mrs. Yoder, whose eyes were starting to tear up again. "I'm so, so sorry Mrs. Yoder, I didn't mean to offend you, but I don't even pray myself, so it's hard for me to think of myself as being an answer to one."

"You don't pray?" Mrs. Yoder said softly. "Well then, it looks like our Sylvie isn't the only one who's in need of help, is she? Goodbye Dr. Brannigan, and thank you again. We'll see you next week, at the same time?"

Kate could not get a word to come out of her mouth, and she just nodded "yes" as she started coughing again. When she finally regained composure, she called out "Wait a minute! Mrs. Yoder! I forgot to ask you something!" Kate got up and went to the door looking down the hallway to see the frail looking woman starting down the stairs. "I forgot to ask you about your insurance?"

"Oh, we'll pay cash. If you can help save our daughter, we'll give you his chunk of the inheritance, he's being written out of the will tomorrow. Don't worry, we're good for it. Fifty thousand ought to see us through this, don't you think?"

Before Kate could utter a word of protest, Mrs. Yoder stopped her by raising her hand in the air as she continued down the stairs, calling out, "Now, before you say it's too much, ask yourself how much you would spend to save *your* child?"

Kate stared at the empty staircase in disbelief. She waited at her office door, trying to make sense of what had just happened; attempting to figure out whether she should be upset about what she just found out about Sylvie, or celebrate the answer to a prayer she never said had just taken place.

"Assume that God *is*," She said out loud, thinking about what Pastor Williams had asked her to try. She looked up at the ceiling and said, "Okay, well then," as she shook her head, smiling.

CHAPTER THIRTY

Fifty Thousand Dollars. Kate could not put the figure out of her mind. How in the world could the old woman have known that number? How could it be that only yesterday Fifty Thousand Dollars was the *exact* same quote her lawyer had given her to pay his fees, the back taxes on the property, and be set financially for a few months? After all the bills were paid, she would have a substantial sum left over. Comfortable for *here*, comfortable for her life *now*. What was once tossed around as the amount for a minor nip and tuck seemed to be worth more than Kate could fathom. She would have to work with a full caseload for months just to make that. She was overwhelmed and frightened about what was at stake. It came down to what she was willing to fight for. Staying here meant dealing with living in some town miles from the nearest interstate, amid corn and mosquitoes and crickets chirping too loudly…and people she was beginning to care about very, very, much. Moving back to California meant she wouldn't have to deal with any of that. The decision was remarkably easy.

As soon as Kate got home, she sat at her desk and got out a pen and paper. She dialed number after number searching for resources and finding people who would help her with her new clients. She was surprised at the amount of assistance available in some places and how few services were available in others. She called hotlines and shelters, hospitals and police stations up and down the eastern seaboard. Kate wasn't exactly sure where the Yoders were planning on sending Sylvie, but she wanted to make sure that their daughter felt safe and had a plan no matter where she landed. Kate smiled and wrote a note to herself to find out directions to doctors, dentists, grocery stores and bakeries in the town Sylvie would be going.

After gathering all the information that she could, she placed the sheets of paper in an envelope marked "Freedom" and put it in her briefcase. Freedom for Sylvie. Freedom for herself. She took a deep breath and dialed Jared Taylor's number.

"Hello?"

"Jared, it's Kate. I've come to a decision. The paperwork is being finalized this week, and the taxes will be paid on the farm. We're staying." Kate was surprised at how confident she felt.

"Alright." Jared Taylor replied.

"Okay then, are we good? You aren't going to try and sneak in anything else before I sign the divorce papers? I mean, because if there is, know that I am determined to make a go of it here. I am happy here. The kids are happy here. You can see them anytime you want, but we are not moving."

"Alright."

"Alright? Just Alright? So this is how it is going to end with just an *alright*?"

"What do you want me to say, Kate? That I am going to keep fighting you? Fighting *for* you? That's not going to happen. I'll sign over the deed to the farm, it's losing money anyhow. Sometimes investments disappoint. You obviously see something there that I don't. Keep up with the taxes and I won't have a problem. Sunny and I broke it off by the way."

"Oh."

"Well. Okay then, goodbye."

Kate didn't say goodbye. She was still trying to figure out if this was all a big set up, or if Jared Taylor really did seem defeated. She knew exactly what he meant when he said investments disappoint. He was taking one last crack at her and she didn't bite. Why did he tell her that he and his mistress had broken up? He did sound sad.

A strange gnawing sympathy rose up and started biting at her heart. Enough time had passed since she left, that she had begun to forget what it was like before the move. She remembered her journal and the entry she read every night when she first arrived in Iowa. She took the key from her dresser drawer and unlocked her desk, grabbed her journal and opened it to the last entry in June of the previous summer. It had been earmarked and referenced so many times the top corner of the page was tearing off.

June 30, 2014

I am writing this so that I never, ever, forget why it is I am leaving. If I actually ever have the guts to leave. I found her lingerie under our bed last week when I dropped my reading glasses and reached down to pick them up. I picked it up and threw it at him. He cursed at me and told I needed to put it in the laundry. I asked him how many times he had her here, in my house, and he just shrugged his shoulders and went to sleep. I hate him right now. I hate him for not seeing me as a person, I hate how he uses the money to coerce and control and I hate how he bullies people to get his own way. Mostly, I hate myself. How stupid I am!

I never smile, I snap at the children when I do see them, which is not often lately. I have been in bed for 4 days straight and no one except for the maid has come to see me. I don't want the kids to suffer, that is the last thing I want, but I don't want to wind up some crazy old woman who everybody talks about but never talks to. If I ever do get the courage get out of here and I feel like I should turn around and come back, I want to remember how I feel right now.

Kate closed the journal and put her head in her hands. She did not cry. She was not sad. She couldn't really decide what it was she was feeling. The adrenaline rush she was preparing for never appeared. It was simple. It was final. No fight. The hours of practicing what she was going to say and how she was going to say it was for nothing. She was so ready for a "*so there*," moment, so looking forward to a "*don't go, I'll do anything*," appeal from Jared and it never happened

After sitting at the desk staring off into space for a long time, the phone rang. It was a women's shelter in a small town in Maine. They had space available, but they could only hold it for one week, they needed an answer from Sylvie within 24 hours. Adrenaline rush wish fulfilled, she called the Yoders.

"How soon can we set up an appointment?" asked Mrs. Yoder.

"I'd say today, but it's after office hours, but that would be might make him suspicious. I will tell you what I think we should do, and you tell me if you think it's a good idea. I think we should just say *yes* to the shelter rather than risk losing it altogether, and then we should try to meet and put together some sort of plan as soon as possible. Can I see you tomorrow?"

"Yes, I think that is what we should do too, but that doesn't give us much time."

"Believe me, I wish we had more time too, but we have what we have, and let's not waste it."

"I will talk with Mr. Yoder, and we'll get a hold of Sylvie, too, maybe take her out to eat so we can talk without him being right there. I don't want to do anything to make him suspicious, but I doubt whether a brunch date would cause him alarm."

"Okay, perfect. Call me in the morning, and do that thing you always talk about doing."

"Praying?"

"Yeah, that."

CHAPTER THIRTY-ONE

Sylvie was shaking, her dark eyes were darting back and forth wildly as she unbuttoned her raincoat. Her parents had a weary and worn look on their faces, yet Kate noted that they were both smiling.

"Come in, sit down, we have a lot of work to do," Kate said excitedly.

"I am not sure, maybe this isn't the right thing to do, I mean, it is not as if he goes around hitting me all the time," Sylvie said, turning away from her mother as she shook her arms from the coat sleeves. Mrs. Yoder reached over to help her take it off and Sylvie recoiled.

"I don't need your help, mom! I don't *need* any of this. Honestly, I don't understand why you are all making such a big deal over this, it's not like my life is in imminent danger or anything, I'll be… fine."

"So fine that you were crying and shaking the whole way here?" Mr. Yoder said.

"Oh hell. Dad, I love you, but you have no idea what my life is like. You don't know what I was crying *about.* You only *think* you know."

"We have time to sort this out, but I need you all to sit down so that we can get started on a plan of action," Kate interrupted.

"Well, I suppose the first thing would be to make sure that he doesn't suspect anything, it's a little late to tell him that we have another appointment tomorrow, but maybe if we could come up with something believable, some reason to come back sooner than next week."

"Like a doctor's note?" Sylvie said, sarcastically.

"Well, yes, a doctor's note...exactly!" Kate replied, hopeful that Sylvie might actually start to participate in saving her own life.

"Mr. and Mrs. Yoder, do you mind if I speak with your daughter alone for a moment?"

"Of course, let's go across the street, sweetheart, I noticed a nice bakery, maybe we can have a donut," Mr. Yoder took his wife's hand and led her out the door.

Kate smiled, consciously hoping that Wally was in the mood to give them one of his "sermons," because she needed all the time she could get to talk with Sylvie, alone.

After the Yoders had left the office, Sylvie's demeanor changed dramatically. She paced the room, wringing her hands and clenching her teeth.

Kate watched her for a few moments then stood up and walked toward her, "So, are you going to tell me what's really going on?"

"I think you have a pretty good idea," Sylvie snapped.

"Actually, I don't. I've met you twice now, and all I know is what your parents have told me. I don't think that's everything. I don't think that even begins to scratch the surface."

"They hate him, okay? They always have. They honestly live in this little dream world where every relationship is just like theirs or it isn't good at all. It's so annoying. Look, my old man is not perfect, but I'm not either. I'm mouthy and mean and don't know when to just let things be. I push and I push and I get smacked sometimes. No big deal, I mean it's not like I am some poor abused woman who can't defend herself."

"Really? Well, you would say that you are happy then?"

"What is the big deal about being happy? How many people do you know that are happy? Other than my parents, I can't think of one person who isn't miserable. They make my old man out to be some monster who is never decent. That's not true. He can be sweet, sometimes. Sometimes we get along great. The only complaint I have, really, is that when he's mean, he's really mean. So am I happy, no. I wouldn't say that. But there are worse things, you know. If I was alone would I be happy? Is the problem really him? Who's to say that if I went through with this little plan of theirs, yours, whoever's, that I would be happy?"

"No one is guaranteeing that you would be happy. If I could promise you that, do you really think I would be in practice *here*, of all places? Actually, I probably *would* be right here." Kate said softly, trying to get Sylvie to relax.

"Well, then? What's the point? Why do it?" Sylvie said sharply. "To make mom and dad happy? To make sure I am not cut out of the will?"

"So you won't die at his hands, Sylvie. Your parents just want you alive. I need you to tell me the *truth*."

"Enough with the drama!" Sylvie shouted. "You think I don't know *exactly* what is going on? You are trying to trick me into leaving. You don't think I want to, sometimes? You don't think that I wake up wondering what I can do to keep him from getting mad? It's my whole life! Could this be the last time I get to sip a beer or go to the movies? If I wear this dress will he accuse me of sleeping around? If I serve this dinner will he throw it across the room? If I breathe will he curse at me and tell me I'm *doing it wrong*? What?! It's on my mind every second of every day. I wouldn't expect someone like *you* could understand. You have *no idea* what my life is like, so excuse me if I'm not too thrilled with letting you plan the rest of it."

Kate was so shocked that she was unable to get her thoughts together fast enough to say anything before Sylvie started in again.

“I'm not stupid, you know, it's not like I just woke up one morning and said “Oh my! Perhaps the person I chose to spend the rest of my life with, wants nothing more than to end mine,” Sylvie said as she rolled her eyes. “God, just look at you, so smug in your perfect little life, that you want to do your little charity work with little miss battered woman. Only I know it wasn't for charity now, was it? How much are they paying you? Whatever. Like I said, you have no idea what it's really like.”

“You know, what, Sylvie? You're right,” Kate said as she walked over to the door and put her hand on the doorknob. “I don't know what it's like to be you. I don't know what it's like to be afraid that someone else might kill me. But let me tell you what I do know. I do know what it's like to want to kill *myself* because of the way I had been treated. You may think I am some old farce, and that's fine. You can go ahead and think that. I can't force you to do anything you don't want to do. I don't want to push you or coerce you into doing something against your will. You've had to live with that every day. Believe it or not, I *do* know what *that* is like. My circumstances may not be the same as yours, but I *do* know how it feels to be faced with a decision like this one. So. You get to choose. Let me ask you this, do you know how many women die every single year that are in the same position you are? Don't answer, I'll tell you. Four Thousand. *Every single year.* Do you know how you are different from them, Sylvie? *You still have a chance.* So. We'll follow your lead. If you want to stay, we can try to keep you as safe as we can, but know this, I'm not going to give up on you, no matter what you wind up doing. However, leaving or staying? Well, that's entirely up to you."

Sylvie looked surprised. Kate was relieved to see that look. She knew that if she allowed the choice to be Sylvie's, she might be less resistant. After being told what to do by her husband, and her parents, Kate guessed that leaving it up to Sylvie would be the thing that would ultimately work. It was, after all, the only thing that ever actually worked for Kate.

"So...for real? What would it look like, I mean, what would happen if I chose to...leave?"

Kate sat down with Sylvie and explained the plan, the resources that were available and how she could stay as safe as possible, whether in the small Maine town or here. The choice was Sylvie's.

"You know that if he ever finds out you are helping me, he will go after you. He will. He told me once if I ever left, my parents would be the first to go, and then he would find whoever else he thought was stupid enough to take what belongs to him and make them sorry. I can't do that to my parents, I can't put them in that kind of danger. I can't put you in the middle of all of this either. It just isn't right, Dr. Brannigan. I made this bed, I'll be the one to lie in it."

Kate winced and said, "You know what, Sylvie? I understand how you feel about that, I really do. Do you know why? Because I thought the same thing. I thought if I got myself into something, it was up to me, alone, to figure out how to get out of it. I am here to tell you, that is a lie that we tell ourselves. Who is to say that even if you stay, he won't try and harm your parents? How can you be sure?"

"I can't, but I *know* he will if I leave. Thank you, Dr. Brannigan, really, but I can't go, I can't do that to my mom and dad." Sylvie stared at the ceiling for a moment then turned to Kate, "How did you get away?"

Kate was startled by the question. "Why I didn't have anything to get away *from*, I am just going through your normal, run of the mill, bitter divorce," she tried to laugh but it fell flat.

"Right," Sylvie said.

"What was that?"

"Nothing."

"I think your parents are well aware of the risks, but if you want me to talk to them, I will. I think you and I both know they are miserable and upset because they hate to see their daughter going through this. Put yourself in their shoes, how would you feel? Sylvie, you have a chance to give your parents some real peace and an opportunity to be safe yourself. I hope you will reconsider." Kate was practically pleading with Sylvie, but she knew she could do nothing more than make suggestions and it made her mad. She did not like feeling so helpless.

"Okay," Sylvie replied.

"Okay, what?"

"Okay, I'll do it. I can't stand to see my parents worry like this. You can keep them safe?"

Kate replied, "I will do everything in my power to make sure they are okay. You do realize, Sylvie, that this means you cannot contact them, you cannot write them, and you cannot speak with them. Not until something changes. He will either trip up and do something to get himself arrested, or he'll do nothing and wait, but either way, you won't be doing yourself any good, and you'll put your parents in danger if you try and contact them."

Sylvie swallowed hard, "Yes. That is going to be the hardest part. I talk to them every day, what are they going to do? What am I going to do?"

"I will work with them and set up a safety plan. Actually, Sylvie, if they follow what I tell them, they will be safer after you leave than they are right now, so, what do you think? Can you do this?"

"Yes. Yes, I'll do it. I actually have friends in Maine, maybe I could stay with them for a while too," Sylvie offered.

"No, I don't think you understood me correctly, Sylvie. No contact of any sort with anyone you know. I can relay messages via a burner phone that I will get you until you get to the safe house, but after that, nothing, no birthdays, no funerals, no contact at all. If he is as dangerous as you and your parents think he is, he is not going to stop. He'll wait til you have your guard down. Do you still think you can do this?"

"I don't know what to do," Sylvie said. She got down on her knees in the middle of Kate's office and started to pray. "Please help me make the right decision and guide me in the way that I should go..."

Kate looked at the woman who had gone from looking like a stereotypical biker chic to a young woman, trembling, and pouring her heart out as if her life depended on in it. Generally, Kate would have been left speechless and feeling awkward. She had never witnessed anything remotely like what she saw Sylvie do, and although it shook her a little, Kate felt more curious than upset.

Sylvie just didn't seem the type that Kate could ever picture dropping to her knees in prayer. Far from being holier than thou, Sylvie freely admitted that she was a more than just a little messed up. She was just a person. A person like Kate. Something about her caused a short circuit in Kate's hardwired sarcasm reflex which would normally cause her to make some derogatory remark about people who talk to God as if He were real.

Judge not, Kate. You talk to me all the time.

"Shh...Gran....I'm trying to think here," Kate said as quietly as she could under her breath. Sylvie was silent, still kneeling, with her eyes still closed tightly.

Look at the world as if God is, Kate, she reminded herself of the promise she made the pastor. She didn't know why, exactly, but it was important to her that she followed through on her word, it mattered to her that she, at least, *try* to do as he suggested.

When Sylvie was done praying, she got up, looked at Kate with a smile and said, "Okay. It's good. Let's go get mom and dad, I hope they are still at the bakery, I could really go for a croissant."

Kate took Sylvie gently by the arm, smiled, and said, "A kolach, that's what you need today, Sylvie, you have got to try a kolach."

CHAPTER THIRTY-TWO

Aside from some paperwork, the plan to get Sylvie to safety was in place. Once she made it to Augusta, the safe house would have all the documentation needed to set her up with a new social security number, a new driver's license and an opportunity to find reliable work. Kate thought back to the time when she had first walked in the farm house with bags overflowing. Shoes, designer dresses, and jewelry were occupying ten bags that were carried in one at a time because they were so heavy. Sylvie would be starting over with nothing but the clothes on her back.

She woke up early on the morning she was to meet with the family for the last time and wrote some directions down to both Sylvie and the Yoders. If any one of the instructions was disregarded, forgotten or missed for any reason, the whole plan was in jeopardy. Kate was thankful that her friends agreed to help. This was one time when Kate knew she could not do it alone, not with so much at stake. Maeve had volunteered to meet the Yoders just outside of town at the rest stop and give Sylvie a car to drive to the train station. Sawyer bought the car, it was just a $500.00 clunker, but that was all she needed to get her there.

Taking the train was a slower form of transportation, but it was agreed that it would be the last thing Sylvie's husband would think of, so it seemed the safest bet. Once Sylvie got to Davenport, she'd take the train to Chicago, get off at Union Station and switch trains. She was to go from Chicago to Pittsburgh, check in with Kate on one of the prepaid phones, then fly out of Pittsburgh and arrive in Maine by nightfall on the second day of her trip, calling Kate when she arrived with another prepaid phone. The third burner phone was to be used only in an emergency. It was going to be difficult, and Kate hoped that Sylvie's husband was as daft as the Yoders had described him to be.

Maeve would use Sylvie's phone to call Triple A to report a flat tire from the rest stop, so if the phone calls were being monitored, it would explain any delay. The whole day was planned around this office visit, and as Kate sat there, pensive, clicking the top of her pen in and out, she thought of how lucky she was that she did not have to leave in any real fear, at least not the kind of fear Sylvie must be feeling. She picked up her cell phone and dialed Jared Taylor. He answered on the first ring.

"Hello?"

"Jared?"

"Kate, I'm surprised to hear from you, is there something wrong?"

"No, nothing is wrong, or at least not as wrong as I used to think. Jared, you *are* an arrogant jerk, but you are not the worst and I *did* pick you, after all. I just wanted you to know I don't hate you and that I wish you the best."

"Uh. Ohhh –kay? Are you *sure* you are alright, Kate?"

"Yes, yes, it's just that I am working with a young woman who is in a tough position, and it got me thinking that our situation could have turned out so much uglier than it did. I just wanted to tell you that. I just wanted you to know...oh man, this was so much easier in my head…ugh."

"Kate, I know it doesn't change anything, but I really am very, very, sorry that it…that *we*, didn't work out. Take care of yourself, alright? I'll be planning on having the kids picked up tomorrow at the house for the flight home. I've got one of our people flying out to meet them and accompany them here for visitation. We are going to have a blast. Goodbye, Kate."

Kate hung up the phone and cried. She never thought she would be grateful for the things that caused the ruin of her marriage, but when she considered what Sylvie was going through, the issues between Jared Taylor and herself seemed to pale in comparison. The tears for herself then turned into tears for her young client.

"Trust in the LORD with all your heart, and do not lean on your own understanding. In all your ways acknowledge him, and he will make straight your paths."

Kate look up at the ceiling, wiped the tears from her eyes and said, "I don't think I've ever been so happy to hear from you as I am right now, Gran. Maybe the way I talk to you *is* kind of like how I should talk to God? I don't know. Watching that poor girl just go to her knees and pray like that, facing what she is facing. The thing is, she actually seems to believe that it is possible that everything can be okay. I just don't know if I can put it into the hands of something that I'm not even sure exists. I'm trying Gran, I'm really trying. I love you and I miss you so much." Kate got up and grabbed her grandmother's quilt, put it into a bag and headed out to her car, smiling. She would give the bag to Maeve, then Maeve could give it to Sylvie before she left on the train. It was going to be a pain to carry around since it was so bulky, but Kate knew that if it gave Sylvie half as much comfort as it gave her, everything really *would* be okay.

CHAPTER THIRTY-THREE

The Yoders arrived at Kate's office on time and surprisingly calm. Kate looked at them curiously and offered them some coffee.

"I would love some, cream and sugar, too, please," Mrs. Yoder smiled.

Kate did not actually have any coffee made, she just offered out of habit, not expecting anyone to take her up on the offer.

"Right. Mrs. Yoder, I apologize, but we're actually going to have to go across the street for that. But first, let's sit down and talk about what we are going to do next."

"We are moving," Mr. Yoder said flatly.

"Really? Was this something you had planned or…"

"Actually, no. We have so many good memories here, we have so many friends, but like Sylvie, we want to be safe, so we're heading out to Kansas City tomorrow."

"I see, well…have you heard anything yet from Sylvie's husband?"

Mrs. Yoder shook her head in dismay and handed Kate the cell phone that belonged to Sylvie. The messages were graphic and vulgar, but they did not imply any threat directly, so Kate eased a little.

"May I keep this as a way to track him?" Kate asked.

"If it would help, certainly," Mrs. Yoder replied.

"We won't be out of the woods until she's in Augusta. From what the safe house told me, these situations can be very unpredictable, but most of the time everything goes okay, at least as far as getting her there safe," Kate said. "Unfortunately, the percentage of women who wind back up with their abusers is incredibly high, so while we can get her there safely, *staying* there safely is completely up to Sylvie. Right now, though, *your* safety is something I am concerned about."

"We agree, that is why we are not going back home, it would make him suspicious," Mr. Yoder said. "We'll be taking the bus to Cedar Rapids and flying out from there tomorrow."

"Kate was genuinely surprised at the calm demeanor that Mr. Yoder seemed to have. "You seem so at ease, I can't help but ask, how is it that you aren't going crazy right now?"

"We have you, we trust you, but ultimately this is all in God's hands," Mrs. Yoder smiled. "We know that Sylvie trusts you too, and *that* is the important thing. She listened to you, she will do what you told her to do. You got through to her, Dr. Brannigan, when nothing we could do seemed to."

"Wow. Well then, that's a lot to live up to, I hope that you are right."

"We need to leave now if we are going to make the bus, will you be able to get a message to Sylvie if she calls?" Mrs. Yoder asked.

"Certainly."

"Just tell her we love her, and that we are proud of her," Mrs. Yoder started to cry, and Kate cried along with her.

"It's going to be okay," Kate said. She stood up and sniffled a little, then walked the Yoders to the office door.

"It's in God's hands," Mr. Yoder said again, smiling at Kate. "No matter what happens, it's going to be okay." He put his hand on Kate's shoulder and shook her hand with the other. "Thank you for helping to save our daughter."

"Make no mistake, Mr. and Mrs. Yoder, Sylvie is saving herself."

"Here you go, don't open this until we are gone, please. Dr. Brannigan, we really should get going, we don't want to miss this bus," Mrs. Yoder handed Kate an envelope, gave her a hug, and disappeared down the stairs as Kate stood in the doorway, crying.

Without looking at the contents of the envelope, Kate gathered her things and headed out the door for home.

CHAPTER THIRTY-FOUR

The call came in at 2 am. Kate had stayed awake, staring at the phone and when it finally rang, she answered excitedly. It was Sylvie. She had made it to Pittsburgh.

"I guess this is it, Dr. Brannigan, no turning back now. I'm really doing this, I'm actually going through with this. Unreal. This is unreal."

"How are you feeling, Sylvie? Did you get any sleep on the train? I think everything is okay here, I do have your phone in case he tries to call."

"I'm okay, no sleep, but I'm okay. He won't try to call, Dr. Brannigan. If he hasn't called by now, he won't. He'll just start looking. How are mom and dad?"

Kate hesitated to tell Sylvie anything about her parent's plan on moving to Kansas City but she did not want to take the chance that Sylvie would disregard the plan and try to call them.

"Sylvie, your parents are on their way to Kansas City right now."

"Oh. Okay. I guess. They had been talking about going down to visit friends for a long time. Did they say when they were coming back?"

"It will be a while Sylvie, but they are safe. We need to worry about only one thing right now, and that is to get you on that plane and to Augusta. You are on standby, so hopefully you can catch a flight out soon. I am so relieved that you are okay."

"I am okay. A good okay. Thank you so much, I could not have done this without your help. Oh! I almost forgot! Dr. Brannigan, thank you for the amazing quilt too! I didn't get a chance to grab the one mom made for me, it's funny, but that is the only thing that would work to calm me down some nights when it got really awful. He'd be screaming at me and I would just wrap up in it and pretend to disappear. He started teasing me about it calling me Linus, you know from the Peanuts cartoons? Anyway, I don't know how you knew it, but just having this, has meant the world to me. Did you make it?"

Kate smiled, "No, I can't sew on a button, Sylvie. It's from someone who was very close to me, and I just know that she would have wanted you to have it. I am glad that it's helping." She could feel a lump make its way up her throat, so she changed the subject quickly. "Okay, so Sylvie...please call as soon as you get there, alright? Oh, and no social media of any kind, understand?"

"Yes, I am henceforth a Luddite, oh well, I might as well embrace it. You won't get a tweet out of me. Get some rest, Doctor, I'll call you in the morning."

The sound of Sylvie's voice was so much more relaxed that Kate could hardly believe she was talking to the same person that had left her office the day before. "Be well, Sylvie, and God Bless."

Kate hung up the phone in shock. Did she just say what she thought she said? She had never, in her forty-two years, ever, uttered that sentence. "Well, how's that for a first? Gran, you're getting to me," she said, laughing softly, as she lay down on the couch and fell back asleep.

When she woke the next morning, it was to the sound of the children running up and down the wooden stairs talking excitedly. They were getting packed for their summer vacation with their father. Kate pulled the covers off of her slowly, trying to keep her eyes closed as long as she could. When she sat up, she groaned. She hated the thought of someone coming to her house to whisk her children away for two months. She had never been away from them for that long and had already tried to prepare a summer plan to keep her from thinking about it.

They would be fine, she knew that. What she wasn't so sure of was how she would fare. Maeve and Wally were busy planning their wedding, and unless she wanted to drink a beer with the local farmers on Friday nights, there was not much of a social life to be found. Now there was nothing wrong with them, they were fine company, it was just not exactly the kind of nightlife she had in mind, because she was used to L.A. nightlife. She thought of taking a vacation but disliked the thought of traveling alone. She was too old for the singles bars and wouldn't know what to do with herself if someone ever actually did ask her out on a date. It puzzled her how she could ever have been so sure of herself in college and so insecure now.

Sawyer arrived just before the kids were due to leave, and he brought them some Iowa Hawkeye t-shirts to give to their friends back in California. Kate laughed softly, both because of the sweetness of the gesture and because she had never seen any of her children's California friends dressed in anything less formal than a collared shirt.

When the car arrived for the children, she hugged them both tightly, surprised at how hard she was finding it to let go of them. They had been so good about all of the changes, so easy going when Kate was melting down, and at times they acted more mature than she did. She was incredibly proud of them and told them so as they tried to squirm out of her embrace. She gave each a kiss and secured them in their seat belts, despite their protests that they were too old for that. After reminding them to call, and telling them to be good for their father, she shut the door. As the car turned around and headed back out of the driveway, she headed back to the house, not wanting the kids, or Sawyer, to see her crying.

No sooner had she taken the towel from the holder beside the sink to wipe her face, than she heard a knock at the door. She knew it was Sawyer. She did not want to see him, rather, she did not want *him* to see *her* looking like this. The Kate that threw a fit in the gym parking lot last fall had disappeared. What was left was an emotional, sentimental, and very confused woman who dried her eyes with dishcloths. She threw the towel in the sink and straightened her hair, checking her reflection in the microwave before she answered the door.

"Hey Sawyer, thanks for the t-shirts, the kids love them! It was very sweet of you," Kate tried hard to smile.

"My pleasure, Kate, I was just checking to make sure you were okay, I know this has to be pretty hard for you, and well, I was supposed to ask you if you wanted to join Maeve and me for dinner. Wally is out of town for the weekend and honestly, I don't know if I could handle her all on my own. She's celebrating her half-birthday tonight."

"Isn't that her pre-birthday, Sawyer?"

"Nope. It's her half. Cake and everything."

Kate laughed, "Well I can't very well say no to *that* then, can I?"

"I am sure hoping you won't," Sawyer smiled.

"Okay, give me a couple of minutes to freshen up and I will be right down, you can wait in the living room if you like."

The phone rang just as Kate had gotten to the top of the stairs. Her first thought was to let it ring rather than race all the way back down to answer it, but she decided it could be Sylvie calling from Maine, so she went back downstairs and picked up the phone.

"Dr. Brannigan?"

"Sylvie? You made it there safe! You are ahead if schedule too, that's great news!"

"It's Bill, Kate, you have to listen to me!"

"Bill? Who is Bill?"

"Bill. My husband, he knows everything."

"What?!" Kate yelled, she could not believe through all the planning and arranging Sylvie's escape, she never thought to ask what her husband's name was.

"Listen, he doesn't know where I am, but mom and dad's neighbor sent me a text. I didn't reply, I know you said no social media, but I trust them with my life, I really do. Anyway, they went over to mom and dad's house to take in the mail and someone had broken in. There were papers everywhere, Kate. I know it was Bill, I just know it."

"Well, at least he doesn't know where you are, and your parents are safely away for a while, but I am sorry to hear about the house."

"You don't understand, Doctor…"

"Sylvie, can you hold on for just a second, I think someone is pulling in the driveway."

Before Kate could say another word, Sawyer raced across the dining room, grabbed her by the waist, and hoisted her over his shoulder, carrying her like a rag doll through the kitchen and into the pantry. The next thing she knew she was in a small, strange room, and was convinced she must have passed out and had woken up in someone else's home.

"Where am I?"

"Shhh, Kate, you have to trust me…*be quiet*."

Kate tried to focus as she attempted to make sense of what was happening. She heard the screen door slam and a man's voice yelling Sylvie's name, and she slowly realized she was in her own house, in a room she had never been in, with Sawyer.

She heard a gunshot and the man yelling something she could not understand. Had it not been for Sawyer holding her tightly, she might have screamed. He calmed her down, and got out his penlight, then motioned with his hands that they were to sit down and be quiet, Kate nodded but stayed standing until Sawyer pulled her down in front of him.

The way the footsteps sounded, Kate thought she must have been somewhere under the stairwell, and when she heard the man run up the stairs just over her head, she gasped. How could this be? There were no other rooms in *her* house, the kids would certainly have found a hiding place if there was one. The footsteps slowed and then stopped. Kate held her breath and waited. She was sitting down with her back against Sawyer's chest.

"Sawyer?" Kate whispered.

"Shhh."

It seemed as if they had been in the room for hours, but Kate managed to wrestle her cell out of her pocket without making any noise and only a half hour had passed. She decided she would wait another ten minutes before she tried to speak again. She felt the warmth of Sawyers breath on her back and smelled the muskiness of dirt and sweat as she tried to turn to show him the cell phone.

Sawyer nodded and whispered. "Five more minutes, he might still be out—." Sawyer stopped talking. Kate wondered why, but then she heard it. Sylvie's cell phone. Kate had forgotten she had taken it as a way to keep tabs on Sylvie's husband. Sylvie must have had an alarm set, and had forgotten to delete it. Kate could hear drawers being spilled open, dishes being thrown about until there was silence. She was afraid to breathe, and felt as if she were going to come crawling out of her own skin at any second if she didn't get up and run away, but Sawyer placed his hand on her shoulder, and she calmed a bit. She may have been terrified, but at least, she was not all alone.

"Sylvie, I know you're here honey, I found your cell phone baby, come out now…I just want to talk." It was Sylvie's husband.

His voice sounded too calm, almost teasing. "C'mon, Sylvie…I paid a visit to your parents today…they want you to come home, you wouldn't want them to worry would you? It would *kill* them."

"That sick son-of-a--," Kate had said out loud before Sawyer put his hand over her mouth. She nodded to Sawyer and he removed his hand and placed it back on her shoulder.

"Sylvie, I mean it. Get out here. I just want to see you, I am sorry, I am so sorry," the man's voice cracked. Kate was amazed at how sincere and convincing he was. It madc her realize just how hard it must have been for Sylvie to leave.

Kate and Sawyer sat there in the darkness, completely silent for an hour after hearing Sylvie's husband calling out to her. Kate wondered why her house phone hadn't started to ring, she must have dropped it when Sawyer swept her up. They were late for dinner with Maeve and Kate prayed she would not try to come check on her and run into Sylvie's husband in the process. Her mind was racing, trying to think of something she could do. Anything.

The LORD will keep you from all harm-- he will watch over your life. "Gee, thanks for popping in Gran, where were you a half hour ago?" Kate whispered.

"Good prayer," Sawyer said as he put his arms straight out in front of him, resting his elbows on Kate's shoulders, trying to text Maeve that they would be late. Kate rolled her eyes and let out a sigh, realizing she had spoken her thoughts out loud yet again. She read the message as he texted Maeve and was thankful *he* was thinking clearly at least. Then she remembered…there was no cell service at the house.

She lost track of time, so she couldn't say for sure when she heard the shot ring out. She could not even tell where it came from. The front yard maybe? Kate didn't dare speak, it was Sawyer who broke the silence.

"He killed himself."

"What? How would you know that?"

"Call it a hunch, Kate."

"Well, we can't be sure, what if...what if it's a trick? He might just want us to think that he did something. *What should we do?*" she whispered.

"I know what I am going to do," Sawyer said, sounding more than a little exasperated, "I'm going to stand up, and try to find more light for us, that's what I am going to do."

In her *mind,* Kate yelled at him, she screamed at him, she pounded him on the chest and demanded that he tell her how he planned to get them out of there, how he was going to make everything okay, how he could find a way to turn back the clock by two days. What she actually *did*, however, was stare at the floor in the darkness, sitting perfectly still…until she looked up.

Sawyer found a lantern and the room was transformed, bathed in the brightness of the light. Kate tried to figure out exactly what the room was. There was a twin bed in one corner, shelves filled with pantry items, a makeshift shower with cement floor, a toilet and a large drum that had some writing Kate could not make out. She could not see a door, there were no windows. Was this some kind of torture chamber or place to stash victims of human trafficking? Suddenly the man outside the door alive or dead seemed safer than the man she was stuck in the room with, and Kate stood up and felt along the walls, frantically trying to find a way out.

"It won't do any good," Sawyer finally replied.

"What do you mean? What are you going to do to me? They will search for me you know, and everyone knows that you were with me today. They'll find you. You won't get away with it."

"Oh, for the love of… will you *please* just hush?" Sawyer interrupted. "You have watched too many horror movies."

"Then what is this? Where is this? And Sawyer, why is this here? You knew about the pantry drawer and now this? Where are we?" Kate insisted.

"Look I'm not going to go into it right now, but it's a safety room. That's all you need to know. You are safe, right? Then, there. That should answer your question," Sawyer looked overwhelmed and angry. Kate's feeling that he would harm her, slowly dissipated and she sat down.

"For the record, I don't like scary movies."

"Okay, then."

"Okay, then. Now, what?"

"Now, we wait. We can't get out of here on our own, someone has to press in the code."

"This is insane! I need some answers, Sawyer, I mean what the...?"

Sirens sounded in the distance and Sawyer moved toward one of the walls and put his ear to it.

"Well," Kate said.

"Shhh."

"Don't shush me, Sawyer, I mean it," Kate tried to whisper but it sounded more like a hiss.

"Shh…sirens! I can hear them!" Sawyer said.

“Will they know we are in here, or are we stuck here forever?” Kate said sarcastically. Seized with fear, she started yelling, “In here! We’re in here!”

‘That won’t do any good, the room is pretty sound proof, Kate.” Sawyer replied.

“What? How come I could hear what was going on outside earlier, and why did you keep s*hushing* me?” Sawyer pointed to one of the corners and said, “Speakers, Kate, right there.”

They didn’t look like any speakers Kate had ever seen before and they didn’t seem to be hooked up to anything, but she believed him. “Well, what about the s*hushing*?”

“I needed to be able to hear myself think, Kate.”

“Oh. I see. So you want me to be quiet and just accept the fact that you accosted me and locked me in a strange room in my own house that I did not even know *existed* before, and sit here and be quiet while a madman is running around my house, looking for Sylvie. Looking for *me*? Sorry. No dice. No way, Sawyer! In fact...”

The sound of another gunshot cut through her angry speech and Kate gasped, even though she was relieved it was not coming from inside the house, not being able to see what was happening scared her. When it seemed safe enough to speak, she asked,

“Sawyer?”

"Yes."

"What just happened?"

"I don't know, Kate."

"I don't mean *out there*, I'm asking what just happened *here*."

"Not now, Kate."

"You are a man full of no answers, Sawyer," Kate chided.

"You are a woman with too many questions, Kate," Sawyer replied.

One hour after Kate heard the last gunshot, she tried to decide between screaming some more and listening to see if she could tell if there were still anyone outside of her house. She had not bargained for her property to become a crime scene investigation, and if the police knew of the secret room, well perhaps Iowa was not safer than Los Angeles after all.

It seemed hopeless to Kate. They had been in the room for well over three hours, and although she tried to fight it, she fell asleep, exhausted from fear. She awoke to find a pillow underneath her head. *It must have been a dream*, she thought, looking over at Sawyer to see if she actually said the words.

"Afraid not," Sawyer replied.

"How are we getting out? Is this going to be like the Friday Night Creature Feature where Vincent Price buries someone alive within a brick wall? Sawyer!! I'm talking to you!" Kate was furious. Sawyer glared back at her and held his hand up to stop her from going further, a rustling noise came from the other side of the wall. Someone was in the pantry. Kate looked at Sawyer for some telltale sign of comfort and found none. They both stood there, frozen. Footsteps came closer to the wall Kate was against and then… *click, click, click.*

The drawer behind the garbanzo beans in the pantry was being pulled out. Sawyer started to yell, "Hey! We're in here! Hey!!"

There was a long silence, followed by the sound of footsteps walking away. Kate had not even blinked she was so frightened and had started to dig her nails into Sawyer's arm. He grabbed her hand and released her grip, then started pounding on the wall, yelling, "We're trapped! Help us!"

While still frightened that Sylvie's husband may still be on the other side of the wall, she was more frightened of being left there trapped and forgotten. She joined Sawyer in yelling. Finally, five beeping noises sounded from the other side of the wall and the pantry door opened up slowly. Kate held her breath and closed her eyes tightly. When she opened them, she could not believe what she saw.

Maeve stood on the other side of the entrance with a guilty look on her face and an empty Snicker's wrapper in her hand. "What? I wanted some chocolate, you were late Sawyer, so I came to Kate's to talk her into coming because I know that if you asked her she would get all scaredy cat and say no. Why were you in the old room anyhow?" Maeve wiped the candy from the corner of her mouth, took a step inside the room and saw Kate. "Oh my goodness! Kate! How did you get in there? Sawyer, what's going on? I thought you said you were closing this thing off?"

Kate pushed Maeve out of the way and ran into the kitchen. The phone was still off the hook and broken glass and paper were strewn all around the room. She walked slowly past that to look out into the yard. There was no trace of anyone having been there. No yellow caution tape, no tire marks on the yard. The scenario of blood and police barricades she had played over and over in her head for hours was false.

Maeve smiled, "Well then, you two…let's get going… my birthday candles aren't going to blow themselves out!"

"Maeve?" Kate started.

"What hon? We can talk on the way to the bowling alley, and I promise I won't let you drink anything stronger than pop," Maeve laughed and started out the door, looking past all the chaos and directly at her still open car door.

"But Maeve," Kate started again, this time, she was interrupted by Sawyer.

"Maeve, we were in the room because we wanted to surprise you, and I have to admit, after all these years, I forgot it was a one-way door. Thank you for helping us." Sawyer put his hand on Maeve's shoulder.

"Don't thank me, thank my sweet tooth, hon! C'mon now, time's a wastin'."

Sawyer looked at Kate and whispered, "Let's *try* and wait 'til tomorrow to talk about this, Maeve doesn't need to know."

Kate's first reaction was going yell and ask him if he had lost his mind, but when she looked at Maeve, whistling "Happy Birthday" to herself as she walked out to the car, Kate nodded. "Yes, it can wait. But we *will* talk about this, Sam Sawyer." She followed him out the door, secretly wishing she was just as oblivious as the half-birthday girl she saw now dancing in her driveway.

CHAPTER THIRTY-FIVE

There was no mention of the cause of death. The obituary just said that he had been a resident for 30 years, was an avid hunter, and was married to the love of his life, Sylvie for 10 years. He left behind his mother, father, two brothers and a niece. Kate rolled her eyes over the "love of his life" part, but still felt horrible that the whole situation had turned out the way it did.

Kate hadn't seen Sawyer since the police took their statement the night of the incident. They snuck away from Kate's pre-birthday party to walk over to the sheriff's office. Kate questioned her priorities by going to the party first, but the officer assured them they were treating the case as a suicide. Despite Sawyer's assumption that Sylvie's husband killed himself when the first shot rang out, it was the last gunshot, just as the sheriff's cars pulled into Kate's driveway, that took his life. The officer went on to say he was genuinely sorry Kate had to go through what she did. There was no interrogation, no forms, just like that, done. Kate was left to go home. To the place where a man took his life. To a place where he could have taken hers. She was going home to an empty house with a secret door that led to a secret room, and no real answers for any of it.

Sawyer was coming over for coffee and Kate hoped he would have some answers. Kate had just finished sweeping the last of the broken china into the garbage when the phone rang. It was Sylvie, and she was in tears.

"Dr. Brannigan, thank God! I know what happened, and I am so sorry; I'm so, so, sorry!"

"How in the world did you find out, Sylvie? You weren't supposed to use anything that would trace back to you, remember?"

"I never hung up the phone."

"Oh, Sylvie!"

"Dr. Brannigan, it's okay. I just didn't know if you were okay. *Those gunshots*. I didn't hear you at all, so I got frightened and used the phone at the shelter to call the sheriff while I still had you on my phone. I couldn't hang up. Dr. Brannigan, I could hear him calling my name... he's *never* sounded that... that...crazed before. I didn't know if you were alive, or if he were alive. He's...dead isn't he?"

"Yes, Sylvie. He shot himself."

Oh, dear God…I…what do I do? Should I come back? Is it okay to stay here now that he's not a threat? I just…I just...I don't know if this is how I should feel, but I am so sad right now…" Sylvie broke down in tears and all Kate could hear was short gasps of air over the phone as she cried.

"Sylvie, the place where you are right now will have the help you need to get through this. I spoke with one of the advisers there this morning and told them what happened. They can let you stay until someone else needs a room, but since you are no longer in imminent danger, they can't keep you if someone else needs the space. I am sure they will help you as you make choices moving forward. You said you had friends in the area? You can contact them now. You can talk to your parents now. You are going to be okay Sylvie. You are going to be okay."

Sylvie sniffled, then took a deep breath and said, "Thank you, Dr. Brannigan, for everything. I know I put you through a lot."

"Honestly, Sylvie, you helped me more than I helped you. Listen, no matter what you decide, will you promise me...no. Could you try and let me know how you are doing? I won't make you promise, I know you will do what is right for you. But please, tell your parents…give your parents…oh just give them a hug for me when you see them, okay?"

"You got it, goodbye Dr. Brannigan."

"I am not your doctor anymore, Sylvie…call me Kate."

"Okay. Goodbye, Kate, and thank you."

As Kate was hanging up the phone, Sawyer came in through the porch door, then stopped and went outside and knocked.

"What are you *doing*? Come in, come in!" Kate said.

"Sorry, I guess I forgot, Kate...old habit."

"Don't worry about it. The coffee is just about ready, you are going to have to drink it out of this plastic cup, though, all the coffee cups were smashed when... "

"No thanks, Kate. I kind of just want to get this over with," Sawyer tried to smile, but his face had the look of someone who was apologizing.

"Okay."

"I told you the room was a safe place, and that's what it is. We have had migrant workers come in, looking for food, some work, a chance...and well, they stayed there sometimes. The owner before you put the room in as a way to keep anyone who wanted to spend the night, a safe place to rest their head. The reason it can only be accessed from the outside is to prevent someone from roaming around the house. There were some issues with stealing, even when the rest of the house was secure, but the door was never actually activated during the day, and at the time, it was used put in to prevent unauthorized people from getting *in*, not to keep people from getting *out*. So the keypad entry was actually put there *for security purposes,*" Sawyer smiled, remembering Kate used the same phrase the night he wrote his number on a book of matches.

Kate thought he was kidding, at first. However, since nothing she had experienced since moving to the farm had fallen into any category she would call normal, she decided it was possible. "Well, I guess that solves the mystery, but it's still, weird, Sawyer, way too *Flowers in the Attic-y* for me."

"I know, and that's why I am going to close it up. I am glad that it was there for us when we needed it though," Sawyer looked at Kate and continued, "Maeve is the only one aside from myself that has the code. If she weren't such a chocoholic, we might still be stuck in there."

"Well thank goodness for Maeve then, right?" Kate cleared her throat and raised her cup up in salutation.

"Thank goodness for Maeve," Sawyer replied.

"She and Wally have been so busy planning the wedding, I am kind of having to fend for myself as far as entertainment goes." Kate chuckled. "I'll find something to keep me busy," she said, trying to convince herself. "Seven weeks will go by quickly, I am sure. The kids will be back before I know it. I've got a few things I could use your help with, as a matter of fact, maybe a place for the kids to wait for the bus, to keep them out of the weather, and some fresh paint on the front porch steps, if you think you'd be up for it."

"That's why I am a hired hand, Kate, you want something done, hire me to do it," Sawyer turned around and nodded his head before putting his hat back on. "Ma'am," he continued as he walked toward the door.

"Have a good day, and…Sawyer…thank you for being my knight in shining armor."

"My pleasure, Kate. Have you given any thought to having the Hayride, Hoedown, and Harvest party here this year?"

"From what I hear, it is a tradition, and who am I to mess with tradition, so yes, Sawyer we can have it here…are you willing to help when the time comes?"

"I'll be the first in line. Have a good day, Kate."

After Sawyer had been gone a while, Kate got up and put her cup in the sink. She looked out the window at the field and smiled, this was the place where she was coming together. This was the place she was becoming whole.

CHAPTER THIRTY-SIX

Although she knew it was coming up, Maeve and Wally's wedding caught Kate off guard. She had only finished writing the summary and diagnosis notes on Sylvie's case two weeks ago and was still finding broken things around the house from the ransacking. Suddenly, she found herself in the middle of the biggest crowd of people she had seen since arriving in Iowa. Not only was it Kate's first time ever being a bridesmaid, it was also her first Kolach Festival. Although it was a far cry from the Hollywood parties she'd attended, everyone seemed to be having a great time.

Sitting on the edge of one of the picnic tables, she heard some of the conversations going on in the crowd that gathered around the food vendors as they waited in line for their kolaches. She didn't hear any bragging; no one seemed to be trying to one-up anyone else. She was puzzled but curious. Everyone truly seemed to be there just to have a good time. No politics, no grandstanding, no strategy. So strange.

"Come dance with us!" Maeve called to Kate after she and Wally had their first dance as man and wife."

"I can't dance to this!" Kate yelled back.

"*That's* what's so great about it! It's the *wedding* that's doing the *crashing,* instead of being *crashed! Whoo Hoo!* So *you* are not allowed to *complain* about the *music*! Now get out here!" Maeve laughed, and took hold of Kate's arms and started spinning her around.

"I have to hand it to you, Maeve," Kate tried to yell above the music, "This is perfect! Instant reception! Live music, beer, and food, *and* you still get to be a June bride? Brilliant! Yay for kolaches! Yay for St. Ludmila!"

"It's almost time to throw the bouquet," Wally interrupted. "What are you now, Kate, single or married?"

Kate wrinkled her nose and shook her head.

'Wally, don't, it's too soon," Maeve put her arm around Kate. "You don't have to listen to him, I'm his wife and I'm allowed to say that now."

"Well I am most certainly *not* going to be the reason for your first fight. I'll stand with the single ladies." Kate gave Maeve and Wally a hug, then lined up with the group of women waiting to catch the flowers. Not all of them knew the bride, however, since it was a public event, once word spread that someone in the crowd was about to toss a wedding bouquet, single women from all over started lining up.

"Looks like you've got some competition."

Kate stopped mingling, and turned around. Sawyer.

"Yes, looks like I do," she said, "I'm not really going to try and *catch* it of course, after everything I've been through this year? Are you kidding? I wasn't sure you'd be here since I didn't see you on the bus."

“To new beginnings,” Sawyer said.

“If I had a beer, I'd toast to that!” Kate replied.

“I remember when that redhead was still working over at Tim Miller's next door to us. That *is* her, isn't it, Samuel? She must be, what, twenty-five by now?” the voice came from beside Sawyer but Kate didn't see anyone until she looked down.

“No, sweetheart, Maeve is fifty now. That man she's with? That's her new husband, Mr. Jowalski. They sure do look happy. Well, it's getting late, darlin', let's get you back home,” Sawyer smiled politely at Kate and grabbed the handles on the wheelchair, turned it around and disappeared into the crowd.

The bouquet hit Kate in the nose as it whizzed by her, cutting her cheek. It landed in the hands of a twenty-something that reminded Kate of Jared's mistress. The last thing she remembered was shouting “Good luck with *that,* Tuesday Wells!” before everything turned black.

“Here, somebody grab her feet and get her over to the medical tent, will ya?” yelled a voice that sounded like it was coming from the other end of a tunnel. When Kate came to, she was startled and started screaming for the medics to put her down and give her a glass of water.

“I *told* you I'm just dehydrated, I'll be fine! Let me go find my friend to take me home!” Kate cried. She pointed in the direction she had last seen Wally and Maeve, grabbed a bottle of water and slipped through the scores of people to the spot beside the loudspeaker.

“C'mon Kate! We're going to miss the bus!”

Kate tried to smile, but the pain reminded her to press the gauze on her cheek to keep it from bleeding. A trip to Doctor Bauer would be in order when she got home. She waved to the newlyweds and walked to the bus. The ride home was a noisy one, with cars passing them all the way home, honking and cheering. Attached to the bus were fifty empty beer cans and the sign “Just Married and Kolached” spread out in big white shaving cream letters.

Kate was too exhausted to really analyze everything she was feeling, but she knew how she felt having just heard the voice of Sam Sawyer's wife. The woman became real, she *existed.* As long as she was a figment of her imagination, there was an uneasiness that crept up in Kate whenever she was around Sawyer. The battle that she was having with herself about how she felt was settled. Her heart hurt, but for the first time since the accident in the Gym parking lot, Kate felt peace.

ଓଷ

There was no way to see it coming. Actually, it was precisely *because* she did not see it coming, that the *Bouquet Attacks Bridesmaid* video taken at the Kolach Festival went viral and gave Kate's practice quite a bit of free publicity. The slow motion close-up of her staring off into space, the flowers hitting her in the nose, and the metal clip at the bottom of them tearing the flesh on her face, was played over one million times within a two weeks of the wedding. She was interviewed on the local news and had an article about her in written up in *The Gazette.* It was not because of her work in psychology, not because of her success in helping Sylvie; that she became such a sensation.

No. It was because Kate had officially become: *The first person to sustain injuries as a result of a bouquet thrown at a kolach festival*. Three stitches on her cheek and many interviews later, the story of what happened to her at St. Ludmila's started to take on a life of its own. Some people believed she'd lost the tip of her nose when the bouquet hit her face; others thought she had been knocked out by the pretty blonde girl who caught the flowers after a verbal altercation.

The first part of the video held a secret. Kate was staring off just before the flowers hit her face, but she wasn't just staring at nothing, it was more than that. Those first few frames were actually showing her reaction to seeing Sawyer, as he lovingly wheeled his wife through the crowd of carbohydrate lovers.

ଓଃ

The kids came back from visiting Jared Taylor, taller, tanner and very happy to see their mother. They spent the remainder of the humid late August evenings relaxing on an old blanket that was set out on the lawn in front of the house. Kate enjoyed the sticky sweetness of the air that mixed with the remains of the slowly dying summer. She loved that the kids brought out empty mayonnaise jars and old metal lids with holes punched through them for the lightning bugs. She started her first garden and marveled at the fact that food just doesn't "grow" without a little help. She had learned a lot, but it seemed she'd barely had time to learn how to properly shuck and de-silk an ear of corn before it was time for school to start again.

Stella spent the remainder of her summer adding to her collection of bugs and butterflies with the assistance of Carla's youngest daughter, who was also going into the first grade. J.T. prepared himself for junior high by fishing and spending time with his friends. Although it took her awhile to become comfortable with the idea of letting him walk around town with his schoolmates unsupervised, she also realized it was yet another sign that he was getting older. As hard as it was for her to face that fact that she was not as young as she used to be, the thought of her children growing up was far more difficult.

On his 13th birthday, she dropped him off at Nice Buns as she went in to get his cake, gave him five dollars and told him "don't go getting into trouble now, I'll be back in town to pick up Stella from Carla's around five o'clock, be here, okay?"

"He's a great kid, don't worry," Wally offered as he boxed up the birthday cake.

"I know, it's just that..."

"You are a parent, all parents worry, but after living here all these years, I am here to tell you, there is not a lot he can find to get into trouble with. Besides, I'll let you in on a little secret, we have glass store fronts for a reason, Doc. We all watch out for each other around here. He'll be fine."

Kate smiled and went around the corner of the counter for a flour filled hug. "Thank you, Wally. I'll be back here later to pick him up." Although she rarely noticed it anymore, the farewell "Nice Buns" greeting had not changed since the first time she had visited the bakery. Walking over to the beauty shop, Kate caught a glance of Sawyer locking up his car and heading toward the realty office. "Hey there, Sawyer! Going over to visit Maeve?" she called out.

Sawyer walked slowly in Kate's direction, and replied, "Yes. Need her to appraise Em's house. It's too big for just me, and I would like to build something smaller and simpler. I was considering Cedar Rapids to be closer to..."

Wait. You're moving? You never told me you were thinking about that. How could you? Why would you? It's none of your business, Kate, remember that. Just smile and say something positive. Grateful for her new found ability to control the thoughts in her head from becoming audible, she said, "Well regardless, Maeve's the one to help, you know. She knows what she is doing!"

"The way Wally tells it, she won't let anyone forget it either!" Sawyer laughed.

"Have fun, and tell her I'll pop in later. I'm going to take this cake home before the frosting melts, it's J.T.'s thirteenth birthday, you should come out for a slice, Maeve and Wally will be there too. Around six?"

Sam stopped walking and turned toward Kate, "Well, I would be delighted to, thank you. I'll wrangle up an appropriate gift for him and be there after chores are done."

Kate smiled and waved goodbye. She had a good friend in that cowboy wanna-be, and she was grateful for that.

ଓଃ

That evening, after the birthday candles had been blown out and the cake had been eaten, the kids set out for the evening lightning bug hunt, Stella always seemed to win that contest. “Because I'm way patient-er than J.T.,” she insisted.

Maeve and Wally sat beside each other with a knit throw joining the two lawn chairs together in front of the fire pit. Kate watched their entwined fingers tap on each other’s hands as if they were sending some sort of Morse Code love note. Sawyer came back from beside the house with an armful of firewood and knelt down beside the fire to put another a log onto the embers, then poked at the coals with a stick.

“Have you heard anything from Sylvie?” Maeve asked.

“I haven't talked to her, but I did hear that she was in Kansas City with her parents. They felt like coming back here would open up too many old wounds, so they are staying there, at least for right now. Sylvie joined a support group and from what I understand, she's enrolled in school.”

"Aren't you a little upset that you haven't heard from her, personally?" Sawyer asked.

"No. Actually, I'm a little surprised, but not upset. I think it's a good thing, really. Means she's gotten healthy enough to start the next chapter, it's actually a good sign."

"If you keep on thinking like this, Doc, you'll be taking over the bakery in no time." Wally laughed.

"Trust me, Wally, I have a long way to go, before I'm fit to stand behind *your* flour covered pulpit."

"Sam Sawyer, why don't you leave that fire alone and sit down," Wally teased.

"It helps me think," Sawyer replied.

"Well, it's driving *me* nuts. If you can't sit still, make yourself useful and grab those marshmallows, I think the kids are ready for some s'mores." Maeve said as she leaned in to give Wally a kiss on his cheek.

"The kids had theirs an hour ago, Maeve, where were you?" Kate asked.

"Oh, I was right here. Anyway, I didn't mean *those* kids. C'mon now, break out the graham crackers, I know where the chocolate is."

Sawyer and Kate looked at each other, smiled and said, "Of course you do, Maeve."

Is this what it feels like to be okay? Kate did not care whether anyone heard that thought, in fact, she almost said it out loud on purpose. She felt okay. There, right that moment, surrounded by her friends, her children happily playing in the yard, and a fire warming her toes and sending embers up to kiss the stars.

CHAPTER THIRTY-SEVEN

The new sign Kate had made for her farm hung proudly at the entrance to her driveway, it was painted carefully enough to be legible, but would up looking a lot more like the signs she made fun of in town just a little over a year ago. It read:

Not in California Anymore, Ranch

As she looked at it, she laughed "Isn't that just about the truth." She and Sawyer had just finished painting the signs for the annual fall produce stand, a small part of the big gathering for the "Hayride, Hoedown and Harvest Party" that was held every year on the property.

"So this is right up there with the St. Ludmila Festival, right?" Kate asked.

"Uh, *no*, not quite" Sawyer laughed as he secured the lids to the paint cans.

"Sawyer, can I ask you a question that I am afraid is none of my business?"

"Don't I get to be the judge of whether or not it's your business?"

"Okay. Fair enough. It's...it's about your wife...I mean having just gone through a divorce, I just...I wondered..."

"Spit it out...it will be dark soon," Sawyer chuckled as he sat down on the side porch steps in front of Kate.

"Why didn't you, I mean, it's been so long since she.... and..."

"Because I made a promise, Kate," Sawyer said.

"But...but...surely you didn't think that this would happen when you said that?"

"No, I didn't think this would happen, Kate! If I would have promised I'd be with her until it was inconvenient for me, or she made me mad, or until it just got too painful..." Sawyer's voice trailed, he looked down at the dust on the brim of his hat, hit it across his shins to shake it off and stood up. "I didn't just make a promise to her, Kate. I made a promise to God. I don't take a vow like that lightly."

"I shouldn't have said anything, I am so sorry. Sawyer, I..."

"I could always have said it was none of your business. You may already know what happened, or at least, have an idea. Whispers are deafening in a small town like this. I don't know if you heard the truth about what happened. Time has a tendency to smooth over the edges or make the edges sharper, depending on who's telling the story. Look, I am no hero, Kate. It happened thirty years ago, but honestly, I wake up every morning forgetting until I look over to her side of the bed and she's not there. It's..." Sawyer took his hat off, rolling the edges around in his hands.

"We had been fighting for about two days about whether or not to start a family. I was against it. I wanted to get on my feet first, travel and have time together. She wouldn't hear it. She was determined to have children, and said that she would with me or without me at one point."

Kate drew in a breath. She was shocked at the revelation. Why was he telling her this? He didn't owe her any explanation. She nodded her head but she really did not want to know what happened. She had become accustomed to "arm's length" relationships, Maeve being the exception, and she wanted to keep it that way.

"At that point I was furious. I just could not understand why she was so adamant. So I told her if that is how she felt, have at it. I was already working two jobs just to put food on the table. It's never been an easy job to work the land, but it was especially hard back then. Banks took property that had been in families for generations. The farmer adjacent to you, Tim? He sold most of his land to The Piper for $10.00 an acre and it was wrapped up into what you bought. That's why technically its rented grazing land, but we don't charge him. Look at me, saying, "we" as if it were mine anymore."

Sawyer wiped his brow and looked at Kate, "We managed to hang on to the land until that time, and I am grateful for that, but my wife's medical bills kept getting higher and higher and it was all I could do just to keep us afloat. To make it through that farm crisis, watching my neighbors lose everything, only to lose ours to hospital bills, well I just couldn't see that. So that's when we put The Piper on the market. I would rather have it sold than taken. Sometimes I still forget it's not mine anymore."

Kate's eyes must have given her away, because before she could say anything Sawyer put his hand up to stop her.

"No one told you, because frankly, no one thought you and your husband would ever actually *live* there. I inherited the airport and the farmhouse from my father, and when you, decided to move in, I promised myself I wouldn't ever bring it up. I was just so happy someone saved it," Sawyer looked down.

Kate could not believe her ears. "It was yours? I am living in your house? Sawyer, I don't think I need to know any more right now, I mean, that does explain a lot, but…"

Sawyer went on as if he hadn't heard Kate at all, "Sara was involved in a car crash."

Kate gasped. She had just assumed that the reason for his wife's hospitalization was dementia, some emotional disorder, something else, but never an accident.

"No one even told you her name did they? Her name was, her name *is* Sara. After the fight, she took the car, saying she just wanted some time to think. It's funny, all this land, and she had to drive to go be alone. She couldn't have just walked down to the creek; she couldn't have just gone out to the barn to be alone. She had to get in the car on a foggy night like that," Sawyer continued, as he shifted his gaze from the sky to Kate. "Sara went off the road and hit a tree head on. I almost lost her," his voice began to crack, "we did lose the baby. Sara was eight weeks pregnant and she never told me. All that fighting about starting a family. She never said that she was already expecting."

Please stop talking, please stop talking, please stop talking, Kate mentally begged Sawyer. Her eyes welled up and she looked up at the sky to try and force the tears back in. She tried hard to swallow the lump that was fixed firmly in the middle of her throat.

"Sara never recovered, though physically she should have. She is lost in that moment forever. All these years of trying, and pleading with the doctors to do more, try more, be more. I was angry with her, but I was mad at myself, mostly. It was a mess." Sawyer stood up and put his hands on the arch of his back, and stretched, leaning into them.

"I didn't tell you the whole truth about the room under the stairs, Kate. The real reason it is there. I had it in my head that I could just take care of her at home. I *wanted* her home. I missed her so much. So, that is...*was*...the real purpose for it. Sara would get disoriented easily, and I was planning on keeping her in that room during the day when I was out in the field so that she would not wander off. I wanted it to be a safe place for her. The doctors told me that it would be too dangerous, she had started trying to hurt herself by that time. I know that most people thought I was nuts. For a while, I thought her doctors might have wanted to commit *me*. At the time, though, I just wasn't thinking rationally. The woman I missed so much was not there anymore. She disappeared the night of the accident. I was fooling myself. Anyhow, it sat empty for a long time. For two years, I couldn't walk by that pantry without crying. Every summer I would get a migrant worker or two looking for a job and a safe place to stay. That's how the room became a safe place for them. The door was never shut on them, no one ever tried to steal anything from me… I made that part up because I was too afraid to tell you the truth. I mean, what kind of man would…" Sawyer looked down and shook his head. "After you bought the property, I had planned on having it sealed off. I thought I might have more time, but then…"

Sawyer turned toward Kate then sat back down on the step. "So. That's everything. Now you know all about me. What about you, mysterious psychologist?"

That was a question that Kate could not answer. Not now. She had not even begun to sort through what she had just heard. "Well, Mr. Sawyer, I am afraid I don't know much about me yet, to be honest. Let me get back to you on that. There's plenty of time to figure that out now, anyhow," Kate said, forcing a smile.

"I'm sorry Kate, I didn't say any of this to burden you. I have had many years to come to terms with this all, and Sara and I are doing okay. I can smile again. Please don't be sad for us, we are okay, really. Hey! Did you just say you'd have plenty of time, as in your staying on here? Well alright! We finally won you over, didn't we?" he grinned.

Wait. He's trying to comfort *me?* Kate thought as she tried to think of something to say.

"Naw, it wasn't you guys, it was the warm winters and sandy beaches," she said, trying her best to act as if she hadn't heard what she'd just heard; trying to act like the little girl who came walking down the stairs after hearing about her grandmother through the floor register all those years ago. "Seriously, though, Sawyer...I am sorry I was so nosy, I didn't want to upset you," she rested her head in her hand and looked down at the ground, wishing she could just dig a hole and dive in.

"Honestly, I have wanted to tell you for a long time. I actually needed to hear myself say it out loud. Helped me realize that my home is here too. It wouldn't help Sara any if I were closer, I can't bring her back by leaving here. So, Kate, thank you for asking, actually. I better get going, though, tell the kids to get some sleep. I'll be back to get the cement slab poured for the bus shelter and I should still have time to get the pumpkin stand set up. I can't believe it's only three weeks away. Should be a lot of people this year, everyone wants to see the movie star from California turned farmer," Sawyer's eye squinted as he looked out into the field that ended in orange light filtering through the thick, hazy air.

Kate sensed something different about Sawyer's demeanor, but she could not put her finger on it. She was sure she had her fill of seriousness, however, and started to laugh. “It's a ranch, not a farm, at least as long as you wear a cowboy hat instead of a feed hat, that is.” With her hands on her hips, she continued to admonish him, “Not *everyone* from California is a movie star, *I'm* certainly not. Unless you count that bit I played in,” Kate threw her arms up in front of her and curled her fingers, “Halloween 32: The Return of the Mutant Kolaches!”

“Let me guess, Kate, you really *don't* watch scary movies, do you?”

“That obvious, huh? Well, I'll be sure to put that on my bucket list.” Kate rocked from side to side moving her hand from her hips to her bare shoulders, as the first hints of chillier evenings ahead gave her goosebumps.

“You know, I've never met a man like you in my life, Sam Sawyer. It's like you walked straight out of some decades old John Wayne Western, and although I can't say that I understand you, exactly, I do respect you. I don't think I could ever have said that about Jared. Believe me,” she laughed softly, “no one has ever told me I was *wrong* for leaving him.”

Kate swept her hair away from her eyes and stared at the same sunset sinking into the horizon, unaware that the light on her face made it clear that there was, at least, some regret that came with that realization.

Sawyer cleared his throat and looked down at the ground. "Well, I'll be. You know, just because no one ever told you that you were wrong, does not mean that you were *right*."

"About what?" Kate asked as she looked down at the peeling paint that covered the top of the porch steps and swept her feet back and forth over it.

Sawyer said nothing. He touched the brim of his hat with a nod, closed the door to his truck and started the engine. Kate stood up and smiled at him, then waved goodbye. Sawyer smiled back, then opened his mouth as if to say something; stopped, shook his head, and with a look of amusement, made an overly exaggerated move to check his rear view mirror before backing up. Kate laughed and wagged her finger at him.

"See you tomorrow, Mr. Wayne."

ઙ૪

Kate helped the children finish packing their lunches for the next day then kissed them goodnight. She was almost as excited as the they were about their first day of school. She was grateful that Sawyer was going to come back in the morning to get started on the bus shelter. Kate read in the Old Farmer's Almanac that a colder and wetter than usual October was expected.

This is Iowa, *after all.*

She smiled as she looked at the house phone, that overly ripe avocado colored fixture was going to stay, and Kate was too.

CHAPTER THIRTY-EIGHT

As Kate pulled the quilt she purchased at the second-hand store up over her arms, she smiled. It was all okay. Everything. Warmed by the love of every stitch that went into the fabric that covered her. She would not have traded the feeling she had at that moment, for anything. Although it wasn't from Gran, someone had poured their heart into it, and just like Sylvie, who was starting her new life over with Kate's quilt to comfort her, Kate was starting over too. She would never have pictured herself feeling like this a year ago, she knew she still had a long way to go and she had a lot of work to do before she was done. It was going to take some time to sort it all out. But not tonight. She had time, there was no race.

He makes me whole again, steering me off worn, hard paths to roads where truth and righteousness echo His name.

"Hey there, Gran, I missed you, that was one of those Psalms, right? Hey, are you sitting down? Just kidding. Maeve has talked me into going to church with her on Sunday. I'm nervous, but I figure just once won't hurt. Besides, I think I owe ya. I get this feeling that I won't be hearing much from you anymore." Kate pulled the quilt to the side, slid off of the bed and knelt down next to it. "I know, I know, maybe that's a good thing—but I'll miss you reminding me of what's important. Guess it's time for me to start doing that for myself, though. I love you, and *I'll see you later.*" She folded her hands, took a deep breath, and said, "Okay. Here goes. You know I am not even sure if I believe in anything, so maybe I'm just hoping that there really *is*…that *You really are*. I was told I have to start where I am, and You'd meet me there. So. *Here I am*. Oh, yes...thank You. Thank You for my children, for angel beauticians and bowling alleys. Thank You for parents who love their children enough to risk being hated in order to save them. Thanks for that fantastic, Irish, red-headed whirlwind, for the minister of bread dough and for the farmer in the cowboy hat. Oh, and God? Thank You very much for kolaches. Amen."

ꕥ

A huge thank you to all who have been such a blessing and helped to make this possible: To Jim and Dori Corcoran (aka Dad and Mom) for being the example of what hard work combined with faith can achieve. To my brother Jeff and his wife, Dre, along with their boys, Fox and Connelly. To my sister Cindi and her husband Ahman, and their kiddos, Keeghan, Delaney, Audrey and Maxwell, and to my brother, Jordan and his wife, Liz; I love you all so much. To all the cousins, aunts and uncles that make up the big ol' Bruggeman/Corcoran crew. I was blessed to have landed in the middle of these folks, and I know it. To Dan, Tammy, Kiery, and Kaylee, for being my family on *this side of the Continental Divide*. To the folks of Manchester, Sigourney and Iowa City, Iowa for making those fantastic places to grow up, and to my adopted family wherever I've been, thank you.

I have been fortunate to call Sandpoint, Idaho my home for over two decades now. I am so humbled and amazed by the creative people of this beautiful town, you have always inspired me to *try*. So...this was me *trying*. To just say "thank you" hardly seems enough, but I do mean it, from the bottom of my heart. Now you know who you are, and if you know who you are, then you know *me* well enough to know that if I tried to list everyone, I'd forget to mention someone and then go around feeling all guilty about it. Besides, there's just way too many of you; it would be like writing a book--and for better or worse, I just finished doing that.

Finally, to my children. Brittany and her husband Steven, Jean-Paul and Simone, and my grandchildren, Sophia, Kendrick, and Sierra. You are the reason I did this to begin with. I love you more than you will ever know, but that won't keep me from always trying to show you.

You are why I am.

www.ingramcontent.com/pod-product-compliance
Lightning Source LLC
Chambersburg PA
CBHW021226130626
46554CB00004B/1386